Living in Bright Shadows

Jean Gilhead

Living in Bright Shadows

Published in 2008 by YouWriteOn.com

Copyright © Text Jean Gilhead

First Edition

Published by YouWriteOn.com

To Garry

and, of course,

my mother

With much thanks, gratitude and appreciation to Ed Smallfield, Julia McCutchen, Martin Delaney-Boland, Mala Tu, Alma Hummingbird, Eileen O'Rourke, Pauline Lomas, Joan Lennox, Lynda Mossman, Moira Allan, Jo Machin, Sonja Vives, Hege Hanssen and Sarah Wilkins, without whose support and encouragement this book would never have got finished.

Contents

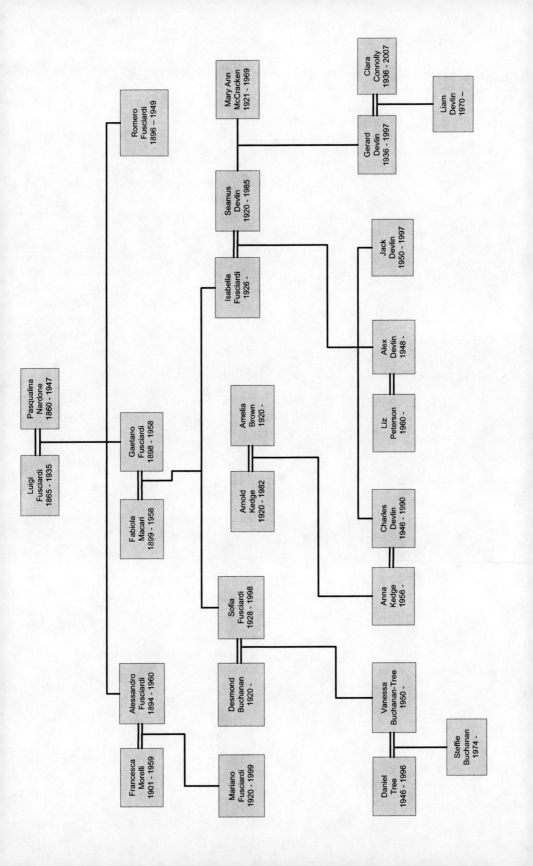

My start was grim; I felt within a growing sense of dread.
Though Mama knew I was coming through, I almost fell off the bed.

What was this place? Whose was the face of the angel that seemed to hover?
It spoke my name but all the same, I felt my life was over.

So off I went and in time I learnt to say and do the expected.
Who could foresee of what I'd be when all around was infected?

Those rules of life, so strange and rife with multi-cultural leaning -
I didn't know they could hurt me so, the rules that had no meaning.

A place of fear, a time less clear brought me to look around me.
Suppose my end, I could suspend in a country that might astound me?

And so I came, three bags to my name, and landed like a winner.
I loved the place, the smiling face of a city like a sinner.

Some times were tough, some really rough as survival mode kicked-in.
But then one day, I'm pleased to say, I woke up with a grin.

I realised behind my eyes was a vision of a future.
A part of Spain I'd loved in vain, that old haunt - Andalusia.

From long ago when I'd dipped my toe into travels far and yonder,
This part of Spain called again and again; the city of the Ronda.

But now I know the path to go to take me to my homeland.
The friends I made will never fade, tied tight round my heart like a band.

by Jack Devlin   Ronda, December 1997
(with apologies to brother Charles, poetry having never been my strong point)

1.
Speck of Dust on the Breeze
- London and Spain -

Jack Devlin - artist - to his mother, Isabella, in a dream.
London, 2007

"Dying was a lot easier than I expected, Mama; it really was just like falling off a log. Once I'd got myself comfortable by balancing one foot on either side of the old Indian elephant stool, it was the simplest thing in the world to just kick it away. That was it; done. And no pain. In fact nothing at all for the longest time and then it was just like waking up, but with no body. You're asleep now but I know you can hear me, Mama. You're in that in-between place that in the morning will make you believe this is a dream. You'll be saying to everyone, 'Do you know, I dreamed of Jack last night – it was so real!'

"Mama, I want you to know that I love the idea of being famous now. If I'd realised it was going to be so much fun I'd have pushed for it when I was alive! By now you'll understand that you never really knew me. Like most people, you went through a sizeable part of my life believing you did, but the fact is that few understood who I really was, what I went through and finally, how I ended up. Tomorrow, when you tell them at the TV studio about your dream, you'll be sniffing and wiping your eyes with those dainty white tissues. You'll have put them into your bag and pockets in readiness for the day. I remember how you'd do that whenever you left the house; 'A fresh pack of Kleenex,' you'd say, 'just in case!'

"And the things people will be saying about me tomorrow (I happen to know in advance, Mama; one of the perks of being dead). I'm blushing a little to think of it. Most of what they say will be complimentary now though ten years ago it was the opposite, once the anger and guilt had kicked in, it being Christmas and all. I can remember how that was too when dearest Michel died in '89; do you remember Mama? I don't think you ever quite realised how close we were. First what hit me was shock and then sadness, then the rage kicked in: my god it was intense. If anger stems from disappointment; well I can tell you I felt blind fury when our Charles told me that he knew Michel had been alcoholic for years. Michel - my oldest friend. We were like brothers but he clearly never confided in me. The day they found Michel choked to death on his own vomit and living in such squalor in that studio, well, you know, that was the day my heart turned to stone against Charles, Mama. That Michel hadn't trusted me with his dark secret was difficult to understand because he was one of the few who knew my secret. But for Charles, my brother, to have always known and never told me - well - that was too much.

"Did you know, Mama, that Einstein said that everything important he ever learned he acquired through intuition? He then spent hours working out how to prove the truth of the intuitive knowledge. As you know, my intuition was something I'd listened to and trusted as soon as I could walk. Do you remember, at no older than three or four how I'd take myself off to explore the streets around our house? I'd be playing happily enough in the front garden then simply get the urge to go. Even then the unknown beckoned like a beacon in the distance. Off I'd go on a different journey and take a new path or direction each time, but I always found my way safely back home again, didn't I? I simply followed the instructions of the angel that sat on my shoulder and whispered in my ear. Mama, you never knew where I was, so of course you went crazy with worry. And when I got back, after scolding me fiercely, you'd fuss and hug me, and plant big wet kisses on my fat baby face. Your Italian-ness couldn't be contained at those times! But regardless of my tender years, Da would simply shrug his shoulders.

"I remember when I was five and I started school in town. It was a three-mile bus ride and you took me there each morning. But I found the lessons so pointless and boring that once I'd had enough I'd just put my coat on, walk out the door and go home. The teachers never saw me go; I suppose I'd already learned to be invisible. There were three or four different routes I could take and I explored each one thoroughly. It took hours to get home but I never got lost or hurt. The reception that greeted me was always the same though: that confusing mix of kisses and indifference, not to mention the occasional police car that was out scouring the streets for me!

"But that sense of knowing which way to go was always with me provided I trusted and relied on it. The angel on my shoulder never let me down. As I grew older, I discovered that people called it their intuition or gut instinct. All I knew was that my angel got me through numerous scrapes and ordeals and out of some potentially dangerous situations. It accompanied me to India, backpacking and alone, even when doctors said I wasn't completely right in the head and I'd get myself into trouble. I remember a mystic yogi once told me that my soul knew I needed to understand and experience the meaning of acceptance, to enable me to come to terms with my childhood years and to move on from them. That made a lot of sense.

"Anyway, Mama, I know you can't see me but I'm often with you, walking alongside or sitting next to you; and I'm always listening. You want to know what it's like being dead? Well, I can see and hear everything now as if all my senses were heightened, the way they were when I was a child. Then too, at night, I could move my body like this, free and unhindered by its limitations and pain. So what if I *was* only a child, barely three years old: I sure knew how to circle the globe and fly to the moon and stars! In the mornings I'd chatter away to you, Mama, trying to tell you about my travels and what I'd seen. But you'd just murmur, *'Si, si, bambino,* eat your toast now, there's my good boy,' while gazing out the window, a cigarette fixed between your fingers. Charles and Alex would ignore my pathetic attempts to communicate and continue kicking each other under the table. And Da would cough and peer at me over his newspaper, looking worried at what I might say next.

"I remember so much about our life then, Mama. For meals, we'd sit in the downstairs kitchen where ice formed inside the windows in winter and everyone roasted in summer. There was the table, slap in the middle of the room, and the coffin-shaped tin bath propped against the wall in readiness for Friday nights. Da would always be first into the water, then you Mama, then Charles, Alex and lastly me. Even then it was as if my small body was of no more importance than to always be there at the end of a queue. Each morning I'd be fascinated watching Da wash and shave at the kitchen sink, water streaming down his arms and across his muscles and dripping onto the green linoleum floor. His aertex vest never came off when he washed, but I suppose he took it off when he got in the bath! As I wasn't allowed into the room at those times, though, I didn't know for sure.

"On Friday nights the kitchen was the cosiest room in the house. You always made sure that the fire was roaring in the grate and the water hot from the stove, because if not there'd be hell to pay when Da rolled back from the pub. By the time it was my turn to get in the bath, the fire would be in ashes and a sad kind of dampness hung in the air. You'd carry me in, all sleepy from the front room where I'd been lying on the floor colouring my Birds of the World book: remember? In a flash I'd snap awake and hop in and out of the cold, grey water as quickly as possible - yikes! There was a tension in the air on those nights and it always seemed to preclude my 'friends' arriving to take me off flying with them.

"In the mornings as I was too young for school, you know, Da would take Charles and Alex in the car he brought home most evenings. All dressed up smart, he'd be, in his chauffeur's uniform. So full of himself, having 'made it' as he said, 'the grandson of a riveter at the Harland & Wolff shipyard.' How he loved to tell the story that his father had told him about the sinking of the Titanic: that if only Great Granpa Malachy had put in that last screw instead of knocking off when the whistle blew, it would have all been so different! Do you remember, Mama, that song he'd sing on his way to the front door? 'Walkie round the garden, like a teddy bear, one step, two step, ticklie under there!' . He'd chase me and lunge forward, catching and lifting me high above his shoulders. Then they'd all leave the house, slam the front door hard and pile into the car as I'd wave them goodbye from the bedroom window. Then you and I would be more or less on our own for the day and that's when my 'friends' would turn up. As I drifted round the house chatting to them, you'd hear me and call out, 'What do you say, *tesoro*? I can't hear you!' 'Nothing, Mama. Only talking to Horsey.' 'Well, I don't know why you call him Horsey,' you'd laugh, coming in through the back door. 'His name's Sam, sweetie, the dog's name is Sam. But he's not here - he's in the garden.' Then you'd flash me a toothy smile and roll your delicious dark brown eyes in one of those 'I do wish I understood you' looks.

"Anyway. As I say, it became a kind of habit, just taking off whenever the spirit moved me. Do you remember how sometimes, after I got home from one of my walkabouts, you'd slap me and send me to bed with no tea? Well then - much later - Da would come in from the pub and sit on my bed and whisper and laugh, and try to make me feel better. Although he never said so, I suspect he could see my friends because he had 'friends' of his own, though his were darker and smelled bad. He made me promise not to tell you about his friends or what they did to me. 'It's our little secret,' he'd say, winking.

"I'd lie there in the darkness, eyes tight shut and not moving a muscle but listening for his key in the lock, then that soft 'crump' as he closed the front door. He'd stagger along the hall and then stop and lean against the door-frame of my room. I remember the sound of how he breathed – like he was struggling to get air down. Cracking open my lids and from out the corner of my eye I'd see his familiar silhouette against the wall. I could smell him, fresh from The Crown, Mama, and my stomach would knot. Then, always at that moment as he sat on the bed, my friends – like horses with wings - would appear and whisper, 'Come, Jack! It's time to go. Come with us. Let's go – NOW!' And as I raised my arms, strong hands would grasp my chubby fingers and we'd be off, flying faster than you could ever imagine. All around us would explode flashes of colour and light; it was so wild. I'd throw back my head and scream with joy, squealing and laughing and wrapping my newly strengthened limbs around my warm, winged horse. Glancing back, I'd see my friends waving encouragement and, as I lifted my hands in the air to wave back, tiny hummingbirds would flit between my fingers, their heads bobbing and changing colour from turquoise to royal vermilion. You know what, Mama? They reminded me of the fireflies I saw in the garden once when Da was helping me count the stars. "I did love Da sometimes. I believed he loved me too because next morning he'd use that special voice. He'd call me 'Da's soldier', and wink in that way that said: 'Don't forget, Jackie boy; it's our secret.' Mama, I so wanted to tell you about our secret but I didn't know how to begin or the words to use to try to explain it. Anyway, you had a way of making me feel like I'd done something bad. Those mornings when I'd wait for you to come into my room, I knew I'd get a slap for not having my pyjamas on. It was a mystery to me how they were sometimes right at the bottom of the bed in a knot and sometimes on the far side of the room: and neatly folded. I'd ask my friends to tell me how my pyjamas managed to get to those places, but they couldn't. They'd just hug me."

Vanessa Buchanan-Tree - Jack's therapist -
to TV interviewer.
London, 2007

"Welcome, Vanessa. I believe you were one of the last people to speak to Jack Devlin on a regular basis before he died?"

"Jack had only ever missed one session with me and he called dead on the dot of nine to warn me he wouldn't be coming that day; it was three weeks before he died. He said he'd had a bad night and was going to stay in bed to try and catch up on some sleep. At the next session he mentioned some new, different, voices that had kept him awake all night. I could tell it had disturbed him but as far as I knew it had happened only the once. So it was strange when he didn't turn up that fateful day ten years ago; it was unlike him. I called his house and left a message, with my number as an afterthought in case he'd lost it or something, and that was how his brother Alex found me."

"How long had Jack been coming to you for treatment?"

"He'd been attending my clinic in Madrid for about three years when Alex called to say that one of my clients, his brother, had tragically died. I'd never spoken to Alex before but I'd heard about him. Some months later he sent me a detailed letter filling in the gaps of Jack's life, and outlining important points. That was really considerate of him because, although I thought I knew Jack quite well, I realised later I'd hardly scratched the surface.

"To say I was shocked when I heard what had happened is an understatement. Jack had been referred by a mutual friend in Granada as, being English, he wanted help from someone he could relax and communicate easily with. It makes a big difference when you don't have to think about the language you're using, especially when you're digging up your past."

"We now know Jack Devlin as one of the greatest artists of the twentieth century, but at the time, of course, he was still unknown. How often did he come to see you?"

"Every Friday morning he'd travel up from his studio in Andalusia; he rented an attic-flat-cum-studio in the spectacular town of Ronda. He'd have his session, stay overnight in a small hotel near the *Plaza Puerta del Sol* in the centre of town, and then catch the 10.30 train back again next morning. In terms of content and progress, our sessions were pretty uneventful because he kept such a lot back. But sadder for me on a personal level was the fact that it wasn't until Alex drove up from Ronda to tell me how Jack had died, that I discovered that we were, in fact, cousins."

"Yes, that must have been quite a shock. So, here we are now celebrating the man as artist; what can you tell me about Jack?"

"Well, he loved the story that his mother, Isabella, told; that he really didn't want to be born so put the moment off for as long as possible. His version was that when he realised he couldn't stay any longer in the comfort of her voluptuous body, he burst out with such force and fury that he shot straight to the end of the bed. Apparently it was only the quick action of a passing nurse who literally caught him mid-air that saved him from a quick finale on the delivery room floor! That story was Jack in a nutshell - subtle but dramatic.

"From the beginning we felt a certain kinship. We were both from London, born in 1950, and both had an Italian mother and an Irish father; of course neither of us knew then that we were related. Before I was born, my father Desmond abandoned my mother, Sofia, and I grew up trying to ignore whispers that he'd walked out when he found her in bed with his best friend. But knowing my mother, that's actually more than likely. It also suggests that I might not be Desmond's daughter; but that's something that to her last breath she flatly refused to discuss with me. I have no idea where Desmond is now, or even if he's still alive. It's been years...

"It seems Jack arrived into a family of culture and sensitivity on his mother's side and abuse, alcoholism and, I'm pretty sure, something bordering on schizophrenia on his father's. I'd heard through our mutual friend in Granada that Jack was artistic but I had no idea how talented or prolific until after he died. During our sessions we'd discuss art and beauty such a companionable way that it brought back memories of my old life in London when Daniel, my then husband, was a photographer and I worked in advertising."

"If Jack wasn't selling any of his paintings at that time, how did he manage to live?"

"Basically, he'd been left all his father's money. It seems that as soon as Seamus Devlin had picked up the fruits of a massive accumulator-win on the horses one day, he'd gone straight from the bookies to draw up a will up leaving the lot to Jack. Seamus died shortly after during one of his drinking binges. The story went that he was reliving the glory of it all and just as he leapt up to open his mouth and yell, 'Barman - drinks all round!' his eyes rolled back in his head and he dropped like a stone. It's hard to understand how he must have despised Isabella and the other two boys, Charles and Alex. But if he'd given it much thought, he'd have realised that by leaving all his money to Jack, he was committing him to a life of estrangement from the rest of the family. On the other hand, maybe he knew exactly what he was doing. Who knows what went on in that man's mind."

"Quite. But let's go back to the beginning. Tell us what you can about Jack's childhood. I believe he had access to some unusual 'friends'?"

"Well, Jack often said that throughout his life he felt he didn't belong or fit in anywhere, because the 'voices' kept him apart and made him different. So it's no real surprise that he sensed from the start that life wouldn't be kind to him. Early on in our sessions he told me that when he was a child his family had lived opposite the big Botanical Gardens near London. I remember early '50s England well; it was a time of naivety and unhurriedness. Although the road Jack and his family lived on was relatively quiet compared to now, it was classed as a 'main' road into London and perhaps one car would speed by at 40mph every minute or so. In those days, Jack never questioned the voices in his head; 'rippling through like leaves blowing in the wind' he'd say.

"Understandably it caused his family some concern when he was young, but the voices guided him safely enough through local streets well before he was old enough even for school. He said he'd be organising his bears in the front garden ready for a tea party, when he'd feel a pressure on his shoulder, and one of them - *his angel*, Jack called it - would whisper, 'Come on, Jack - let's go for a walk.' So, with his favourite teddy under his arm, he'd click open the gate and go, ever ready for adventure and the open road even then. He said that the voices always led him safely across roads and back home again. Of course Jack didn't realise that other people couldn't see the shadows and mists that surrounded him, urging him this way or that, thickening and blocking his way until a bus or car had safely passed. Neither did he wonder if others could see the colours around people that told him if they were happy or sad, angry or lying. Or in the case of plants and animals, sick.

"So, in this isolated world that Jack inhabited, no-one but him knew about the strange, gentle creatures that hummed around and flew with him, high above the houses and street lamps when his father came into his room at night. At those moments, he said, his friends would appear from inside his head and stand there waiting patiently with open arms, ready to whisk him away until morning. According to Doctor Fitch, the family GP who often visited him at home, Jack lived so much in his head that he couldn't be trusted to tell the truth."

"Could his childhood be considered normal in any way, as far as you could tell?"

"When he was very young, he became sick with a mystery illness that put him in bed for weeks at a time and left him unable to move or breathe properly. Once he was even rushed to hospital and had to spend the night in an oxygen tent, he was so ill. But lying there on his back in the big bed in Isabella and Seamus' room, he would watch the clouds slide by the window and imagine he could see animals and children out there. No-one could fathom what was wrong with him, and back then no-one thought to check what now would probably be quite obvious.

"He once told me of the sheer terror he'd feel on hearing Dr. Fitch climbing the stairs to his parents' bedroom while he was lying there. Apparently, the doctor would sing out the nursery rhyme 'One, two, buckle my shoe' as he climbed each stair until he reached the top. Jack reminded me of that nursery rhyme from my early childhood too – I think I remember how it goes. *One, two, buckle my shoe. Three, four, shut the door. Five, six, pick up sticks. Seven, eight, lay them straight. Nine, ten, a big fat hen. Eleven, twelve, dig and delve. Thirteen, fourteen, maids a'courting. Fifteen, sixteen, maids in the kitchen. Seventeen, eighteen, maids a'waiting. Nineteen, twenty, my plate's empty!* Poor man, he was probably only trying to make his presence felt early, rather than just walk in and surprise Jack.. But by the time he'd reached the top stair and opened the door to the bedroom, Jack would be under the covers right in the middle of the bed and shaking with fear. Isabella would tell him off for being such a baby and wasting everyone's time, but short of ripping the covers off him, there was nothing she could do. Jack couldn't explain his fear that Dr. Fitch might do the same to him as his father did. After all, Dr. Fitch and Seamus seemed similar; they were about the same age, wore the same kind of suits and had their hair in the same style, as the majority of men did in those days., of course. Dr. Fitch even smelled of stale tobacco when he leaned over Jack to examine him. I sometimes wonder what Dr Fitch would have made of our sessions.

"But apart from all that, Jack's very earliest childhood years were spent running free amongst the century-old palms and exotica in the Botanical Gardens near his home. Depending on the time of year, Jack, his mother, and brothers would make for the bluebell wood or the crocus patch, or watch the enormous carp swimming around in the pond. His favourite place was the tropical Palm House with its 'comforting roundness,' he'd say, ' like an upturned boat' , and its imposing stone guardians lined up along the front. The statues both terrified and fascinated Jack. He believed that those animals like the griffin (part lion, part eagle) existed and would come to life if he closed his eyes or turned his back on them. But he said they ignored him and 'continued their regal surveillance of the ornamental pond,' where black and white swans built their nests and tended their chicks. After scaring himself half to death peeking through his fingers for movement from the griffin, he'd apparently run to the back of the Palm House and find comfort wandering amongst the formal rose gardens and sculptured hedges, the voices in his head calming and soothing him.

"Day after day, when the weather was good, he and his brothers would roll down grassy hillsides, feed the ducks with enormous pieces of stale bread, chase the red squirrels and hide amongst the heavy, overhanging weeping willows. It sounds idyllic, doesn't it? Who could have know what was lurking behind the façade of that happy family life. Also, there in the Gardens, Jack told me he felt himself hypnotised by the haunting call of the peacock. In later years, in India, he said the sound would draw him back to those days of lost innocence, and drive him to the madness that gave birth to his creative expression: his painting.

"I remember those fabulous Gardens from when I lived in London, and they were always notorious for concealing lost children. I guess this haven was his saving grace when things got really bad at home and, ultimately, his initial preparation for the work that we now know him by. He once said he spent so much time in the Gardens that the familiar clunk of the heavy metal turnstile became the entrance to his own private world, and he believed they were an extension of his own garden. When he wrote his first composition at primary school, while the other kids painstakingly wrote three or four lines, his essay was a kaleidoscope of text and colour. Clearly a taste of what was to come!

"But Jack said his most vivid memory of the Gardens was the atmosphere of peace and tranquillity. Then there were no aeroplanes or cars to be heard anywhere. He'd recall foreigners strolling past and politely greeting him in unknown tongues, 'their clothes and mannerisms exotic,' he say, 'their skins of every shade.' Jack was a storyteller. In later years, through his painting, he'd call up the exquisite colours of the orchids he saw there, the African violets and the birds of paradise; all the psychedelic mixes of pinks, purples and oranges, intense electric yellows, vivid blues and startling reds. To Jack's artistic eye, and in post-war England, they were just a joy beyond words."

"What else did you know about Seamus, Jack's father?"

"Jack rarely talked about his father; or of the violence, the drinking and gambling. Or of how he'd endlessly and cruelly be compared and preferred to his eldest brother, Charles. It set up a rivalry between the two that lasted to the end of their lives. But in our sessions he didn't go there much because it caused him such distress that it affected his breathing. There in my office he'd try to recall happy days as much as possible.

"The only story he did mention a couple of times was about one Christmas Day. Some kittens had been born in the morning and Seamus had come back from the pub in such a blinding rage having lost at the horses that he proceeded to tear down and stamp on every paper decoration that Jack and his brothers had spent the past week making and hanging. From such happiness at witnessing the birth of the kittens to inexplicable terror in just a few hours, well, it left Jack with a deep loathing – I'd go so far as to say a fear - of everything to do with Christmas."

"Did Jack ever speak about any friends? Would they have been a source of inspiration for his painting, do you think?"

"In all the time he came to me for sessions, the only friend Jack mentioned was an English-language teacher from New York called Dan, and Rosa his Spanish wife. They lived in the same town as him. I think Jack had a bit of a crush on Rosa as he often hinted that she reminded him of his mother, but he was much too shy to come right out and say it. Dan was a few years younger than Jack and a bit of an ex- barfly by all accounts, but good company nonetheless. They'd meet most mornings for breakfast, discuss who was thrashing who at football, scour the dailies, rubbish the politicians; you know the stuff. I think Dan and Rosa might have been Jack's only friends; I'm sure very few people really knew him. He was fond of saying, 'We spend our lives living in bright shadows.'

"I wish my daughter Steffie could have known Jack. He was her uncle after all."

Extract of a Letter from Alex Devlin –
Jack's middle brother - to Vanessa.
London, 1998

I've often heard it said that those who are cruel to animals tend to be cruel to people. So you would think the reverse to be true, but in our father's case, no. Father loved birds and small animals; he especially loved budgies. At any one time half a dozen would be flapping round the house like one day they might be free and had better get in as much practice as possible! Many more would be lined up in their cages, their long claws wrapped around wooden perches, watching and waiting for their big break. It was rather spooky seeing them like that, actually. New ones would be born, hatched at night, and we'd come down for breakfast to find more straggly pink life forms with weird alien-shaped eyes.

It was the same with the kittens; one particular Christmas morning was a 'Jack moment' I'll remember all my life. He'd been the first up as usual and, following the sounds of mewing and whispering, I found him gazing down at Susie Two who'd tucked herself comfortably into the airing cupboard. She was thoroughly and rapidly washing three newborn kittens, each the size of a mouse. We were so entranced at this that we just sat quietly watching, absorbed in the miracle before us. When Mother came down and asked what was happening, Jack could hardly speak. With shining eyes he jumped up and started rearranging the furniture around the cupboard to form a protective barrier against the dogs and the rest of the family. It was amazing that such a little boy would think of doing that. Anyway, what I'm saying is that kittens, budgies, hamsters, mice, puppies, any small animals were commonplace in our 3-storey house. Curiously, Father had infinite patience with small vulnerable animals: but with people and children in general, none whatsoever.

As you know, Vanessa, we lived on a main road overlooking the Botanical Gardens. Every day after work Father would go straight upstairs and change his clothes, hanging up and brushing down his chauffeur's uniform in readiness for the next day. He'd never let Mother or anyone else touch it; somehow it was as if that uniform embodied his very identity. He'd then go into his back room on the middle floor and shut the door on the rest of us until supper-time. Sometimes he'd refuse to let anyone in; even Jack was banned. At those times, Mother would say, 'Keep out of your father's way,' for she'd learned from experience that his silence and desire for solitude was a sign, a warning that a volcano was about to erupt. Everything would be quiet and peaceful for a while, lulling us into a false sense of security. Then, when everyone's back was turned and we'd stopped paying attention, father would explode and wreck everything in his path. At these times Jack would hide, but Father would find him and carry him in to where the rest of the family were waiting, rigid with fear. Mother often said in later years that Jack was the 'lucky one, the pampered prince,' she called him, 'Da's special boy,' because he was never physically harmed during these outbursts of violence. Father's rage would mostly be taken out on poor old Charlie who could do nothing right.

The pattern was always the same. First the stillness, the eerie quiet that fell upon the house and caused everyone to whisper and tiptoe around. Then, after an unbearable few hours, the door to Father's room would fly open and crash against the wall with a force that sent dogs and cats scurrying for cover. We'd hear fierce hammering on the stairs as he pounded up and down, two at a time, searching, finding and grabbing each of us and dragging us into the basement kitchen: the battlefield. Lastly he'd find Jack, curled up tight under a bed or tucked amongst Mother's perfumed dresses at the back of the big wardrobe. Sometimes he'd find him sitting on damp earth between rows of green beans at the end of the garden, chattering away to his invisible friends. Jack told me many years later that Father would smile at him and say 'There y'are my sweet boy!' and gently pick him up and, with Big Ted clutched to his tiny chest for comfort, carry him into the kitchen and place him on the table in the middle of the room.

We knew what would come next because it was always the same. First Father would swear at Charlie and call him names and start goading and prodding him hard with his knuckled fist. Then, when Charlie reacted and retaliated, Father, in a state of foaming fury, would shout, 'Right!' and take off his leather belt and start hitting him with it. The blows fell everywhere. On poor Charlie's head or body, it made no difference. Father seemed oblivious to the pain he was causing. I suppose by then he'd been taken over by his 'demon', a dark and twisted creature that seemed to force its way through him, contorting his face and body and bestowing savage strength upon him. Unable to hold herself in check any longer, Mother would spring forward to protect her son, only to find herself included in the assault. This, of course, was what Father had been waiting for so he could then focus his energy on attacking her. As for me, only two years older than Jack, well I'm ashamed to say I just stood by quietly crying, short grey flannel trousers already damp, unable to comprehend what was happening around me.

I knew, however, that by this point Jack would have retreated into his head because he'd be giggling. Knowing him he was probably remembering something like the newest kittens and how warm and soft they felt when Susie Two allowed him to put his hands in the basket and stroke them; animals always trusted our Jack – he had a special way with them. But out of the corner of my eye I could see Father's face, grotesque and red and sweating; spittle flying from his mouth and his false teeth in danger of following. For Jack, I think all would have been silent by then. The look on his face told me he believed he'd become invisible. Once, years later when we were having a drink at my Club, he told me the reason he'd started giggling at those moments. He said it reminded him of when we were at Saturday picture matinees when the sound system broke down and the soundtrack suddenly stopped but the action continued. All the kids would start cheering and shouting and throwing things, then suddenly it would be back on again at full blast until the operator could adjust it. It actually was hilarious.

Jack once told me that, for him, this internal silence was bliss because when he closed his eyes it was like nothing was happening, he was somewhere else; Father was not hurting Mother and Charles, and I was not sobbing uncontrollably. But Jack would then be shaken out of this private world as Father strode over to the kitchen table where he'd carefully placed him out of harm's way. He'd pick Jack up in his arms and carry him, like a trophy, to where Mother and Charlie were standing, shaking and holding onto each other, near the door.

'This wee boy,' Father would bellow, 'this wee boy has more sense in his little finger than you'll ever have in your whole bloody BODY!'

I really feared at this moment because the look of hatred on Charlie's face transferred itself backwards and forwards from Father to Jack.

'This child is smarter and cleverer than you'll ever be, you trash!' he'd roar, raising his arm so the back of his hand caught Charlie across the mouth, sending him staggering. I'd try not to look at Mother, whose face by this time would be puffed up and turning the same pink and purple as her dress, the fabric having been ripped across near the shoulder or somewhere. And her jet-black hair, so beautiful that morning, sticking out at strange angles, as if someone had been yanking at it.

By now I'd have retreated to the farthest corner of the room and, Jack reminded me years later, be hovering by the cooker; fat and ignored. With my arms tight by my sides I'd just stare straight ahead in a kind of trance. Nobody would say a word or hardly breathe. Charlie, defiant again, would be looking directly at the floor in front of him as if he were hatching a plan; the tension in the room unbearable. Then, as suddenly as it had begun, it was over. It felt like when Mother pulled the plug in the sink and all the lovely warm water round my legs disappeared. Father would stand looking thoughtful for a moment, then bend down and pick up his belt from the floor, inspect it and buckle it back around his waist.

'Get this bloody lot cleaned up, you greasy whore!' he'd hiss at Mother. Then disappear up the stairs, on his way grabbing his white silk scarf from the hook on the wall, then out of the house slamming the front door. And Jack would continue to sit wherever Father had placed him, looking uncomfortably around him for reassurance. He told me later that he didn't know where to look; sensing that everyone in the room hated him but not knowing why. He wished he could have talked to us and explained that it wasn't his fault and that he never wanted any part of it. But he was hardly more that a baby, he hadn't yet learned how to turn thoughts to words or to express his feelings. All he knew for sure was that later, while he was sleeping, Father would come into his room stinking from the pub and, with his shadowy friends, sit down gently on his bed and start whispering.

Isabella Fusciardi – Jack's mother - to TV interviewer.
London, 2007

"Please tell us a little about your background and your early life with Jack's father."

"Well, you know my dad Gaetano, he was a lot like my Jacko: gentle, sensitive, a real looker of a man, he was, with thick dark hair and flashing eyes. 'Gorgeous Guy' they'd shout after him as he sauntered along the street. My mother, Fabiola, she used to say the girls fair dropped at his feet! My dad and his brothers, Alessandro and Romero, they'd been sent to Ireland for a better life when they were just wee boys, dad being the youngest. About 1900 I suppose it was. They often said that their father, Luigi, kidnapped them to spite their mother. He just put them on the boat one day with some relatives and they never went back. My mother's parents had been farmers but they couldn't get the land to work for them so they all came across from Casalattico; emigrated, you know. I think they went back a few times, just visiting. If there are any family left in that part of Italy now, well I don't know of them.

"The boys first lived in York Street I believe then moved to Crumlin Road, and when my dad grew up and married my mother, they opened up a fish and chip shop there. Mother and dad lived in Belfast till they died but my uncles, Alessandro and Romero, they moved to London early on and started up Fusciardi's Ice Cream Parlour. I hear say it was a huge success from day one. Uncle Romero died a bit later, I don't exactly know what happened, but Uncle Alessandro had a son, Mariano, who continued running the place well into his sixties. We kept in touch, but he was never been happy after his wife died so he sold the business.

"Well, when I was 16 I married the local wide-boy, Seamus Devlin; 'Shameless' he was called! Everyone knew him, for sure. He wasn't so tall or strong, but he had these cornflower blue eyes and blonde hair with a real cheeky cow's-lick at the front. He was a charmer all right. I had a younger sister back then too, Sofia her name was. In the forties we all moved to England with Des Buchanan, Seamus' best friend. For a long time I missed Ireland, especially Belfast which was grand; surrounded by low, green hills and wide clear skies. I hated London; it seemed even noisier and dirtier in those days. But I grew to love where we lived, opposite some big gardens just on the outskirts.

"After three 'miscarriages' – well, you have to understand we didn't have tuppence between us and Seamus out of work, you know - I gave birth to my three boys in quick succession: Charlie, Alex and Jacko. But my sister, she had an affair I suppose you'd call it, with my husband, which led to a falling out between Sofia and me. She always was loose, that one - what they call a 'right wee goer' back in Belfast. But she was fun and outgoing - not like me, quiet and shy and wouldn't say boo to a goose - so she made friends easily and had a ton of them. Hurt beyond words I was: my sister and my husband, you can imagine. I vowed never to have her name mentioned again."

"And Seamus?"

"Seamus? Well you know he was a creative man by nature, like my Jacko, but he liked to say it was stifled by his hard upbringing. And he was one of ten children. As he grew up I suppose he had to learn to be charming and superficial to get anywhere. He could sweep any woman off her feet with his blarney, that's a fact. But he was too envious of others' natural gifts and success and took great delight in setting Charlie and Jacko up against each other. He was a heavy drinker and a gambler too: the horses were his downfall. He had one big win and left the lot to Jacko when he died.

"He was no saint, my Seamus. When he was 16 he had a fling with Mary Ann McCracken from up the town; her pa was one of the big mill owners. I remember her well enough, pretty wee thing she was, coal black hair that reached down past her bum and the bluest eyes. A bit simple though and anybody's of a Saturday night and a jug of beer. Well, once Seamus set his eyes upon her he got her up the club right enough and they had a wee boy; called him Gerard. They say, at first Seamus took his responsibilities as a dad quite seriously, her father made sure of that! But then when Seamus and I got hitched and came across to England, he never saw either Mary Ann or the boy again. She wrote us a few times, over the years, saying what a good lad he was and that he'd never leave her on her own. Then one day we heard she'd died and Gerard had gone straight out and got wed before her body was barely cold. He got the big house, you see, so he did real well for himself, in the end."

"What about your sister, Sofia?"

"Sofia. Well, she's gone now and, as I said, we never had any more contact after I kicked her out.. She was a cracker all right though, when she was young. Wild dark hair and the palest hazel eyes - 'miele' - honey eyes - they say in Italy. Well, as much as he was mad in love with her, Des walked out and never came back once he found out about her and Seamus – the boys had been best friends since childhood, you see. It fair broke his heart and he never forgave Seamus either. We heard he went back to Belfast and picked up his old job behind the bar at the Duke of York in Commercial Court. But it served Sofia right when Des walked out, the trollop! In fact all her life she was never anything but a trollop. Always flirting she was with any bit of trouser that found itself in her path. "Sofia was two years younger than me and I'd always had to look out for her and get her out of scrapes. Well this was one too many. She and Des had only been wed a year when she set her sights on my Seamus. I was at the doctor's that day learning I was pregnant with Jacko when she charmed her way into our bed. And then, well, we weren't surprised to hear she had a daughter nine months later, even though she was forever complaining that Des wasn't up to much in that department. Truth to tell I've tried not to think about this girl walking around with my husband's stamp on her. We heard through the grapevine that Sofia brought the child up by relying on her network of friends, doing menial jobs and turning the odd trick. She must have fallen on her feet quite quickly though because one day we heard she'd become the 'companion' to some big oil tycoon and that she and the wee girl had moved into a life of luxury in a fancy Mayfair apartment!"

"It seems nobody really knew Jack as well as you, can you give us some anecdotes?"

"My Jacko, he was always a sensitive boy. As he grew up, whenever he saw children being shouted at or abused in the street, well it fair made him tremble. I remember once, when we were sitting in a restaurant somewhere in London, we saw this tiny girl outside in the street – no more than three years old she was – being bawled at by this great ugly bear of a man because she was crying for her mam. The man, he was ridiculing her and mimicking her way of crying, 'Mummy! Mummy!' in a real repulsive and sarcastic way. Then, he just walked right away from her, leaving her alone right there on the pavement. Desperate and terrified she was, poor wee thing. I couldn't believe what I was seeing. I felt my stomach lurch and tears start to sting my eyes, but my Jacko he was nearly choking and I thought, 'my god, he's going to have one of his turns'.

"My heart it went out to the little one in the street but I was so shocked I couldn't move, not for her, not for Jacko. It was all Jacko could do to not go outside and confront the man and find out what on earth he thought he was doing, treating a wee child that way. Well, he was on the point of doing just that when the mother she appeared; it looked like she'd been shopping by the bags she was carrying. But the brute he just sneered at the child and shouted 'Oh, look! Here's your precious Mummy - she's back. Are you happy now, you cry baby?' His disrespect for this tiny wee thing and the violence in his voice and bearing, my god it was awful. And the little girl by this time she was just plain terrified. It was bewildering what was happening, you know, what we saw there: an awful moment, and it left poor Jacko hardly able to talk for days.

"And I asked myself, what kind of pleasure could that have given to that man? Who was he? The father? The boyfriend? How is it possible that a grown man can feel so insecure around a wee child that he would resort to that kind of behaviour? I'd never seen anything like it. But, you know, Alex said it was the kind of thing that Seamus would often do to Charlie, but I have to say I don't remember it.

"My dad, he was a good judge of character, and he loved Seamus; he used to say he was a real good man. He could see right into a man's soul, my dad, and he never had a bad word to say about Seamus. But he must have struck a bad chord with Jacko because it seemed the more he witnessed any kind of bullying behaviour towards children, the more he went further and further inside himself. Eventually he stopped watching the news on TV and, apart from reading about football, which he loved, gave up newspapers altogether.

"Well, now my youngest boy's famous and the world can see he was a bit of a child himself. And sometimes selfish, I thought he was with his hoity-toity lifestyle in Spain, compared to poor Charles in his scruffy studio in Paris. I don't know why Jacko never had much confidence; in fact his father used to hold him up as some kind of shining example, to the detriment of my other two. Those boys, you know, they really suffered; my Charlie took to the drink; and Alex, well he's never been able to stop himself eating, really. I shouldn't be saying this but my Jacko, he just seemed to drift through life with no real sense of purpose – nothing had much meaning for him. He was always a little 'viziato', we used to say; spoilt, you know. But he denied it. He'd say, 'How can someone who has never had sight know what it's like to see?'

"But, you know, my Seamus wasn't such a bad husband, as they go. Hardly ever laid a finger on me, except when he'd had a drink or two. And he'd put his earnings straight down on the table regular as clockwork of a Friday, then take back just a little for the horses. Often they didn't, but sometimes they'd come up. I don't remember Jacko complaining, though, when he was left everything in his Da's will. Poor Charlie never got a bean and refused to take handouts from his brothers even though we all knew he and his wife were going through hard times."

"Can you tell us what happened to Jack's money when he died?"

"Well, you know, my Jacko he did the strangest thing; he turned round and left it all to Anna, Charlie's widow. Then the last I heard she disappeared off to India and disposed of the lot amongst her animal and children's charities and the like.

"Seamus, to his credit after that incident with my sister, he never messed around with another woman; well, if he did he never turned it into a drama. What else is a man to do when he's been working hard all week, I say? He deserves a bit of fun and a dowdy housewife can't expect to satisfy a red-blooded man like my Seamus was. But Alex he tells me I don't remember what kind of bully his father was. He says there was no foundation to Jacko's life, no base or solid ground, no real support for him. Well, I don't know about that, but sure I feel guilty. I was his mother and mothers are good at guilt, especially Italian ones! But it was all such a long time ago now and I did my best. I still feel somehow that maybe it was my fault, what happened in the end.

"When Jacko returned from India, as I said, he started to act like a child. With a child's responses, weak, you know, not manly. He was seeing a psychiatrist I think, a woman in Madrid, but I don't think she was helping much. He once told me that he saw so many terrible things in India that later, waking up in the morning, tears would bubble up from old memories, childhood memories, and he'd start to choke. He used to say he couldn't breathe, like when he was a child. And he always wore the dark glasses, even at night, even though his eyesight was not always so good. He told me it made sure no-one could see the tears he cried as he walked through the streets, just reliving again and again the scenes he'd seen or heard about.

"I find it too hard these days to think much about Jacko as he was never an easy boy, or Charlie my number one. My boys, my first and last, it was all so long ago. But I still have dear Alex. He and Liz, and sometimes even my grandsons, come to visit. Thank god I've still got them to look after me."

A Letter from Dan Kennedy – Jack's friend -
to Vanessa Buchanan-Tree.
Ronda, 2007

Dear Vanessa
    One freezing Christmas night ten years ago, my buddy Jack offed himself. He'd been talking for weeks about death and what might be beyond it, and somehow reached the conclusion there'd be nothing but peace and silence, a kind of drifting through space with all thoughts and memories gone. He said everything would just disappear, as easily as the life force of the body slipping away. Between discussing the latest Barça and Real Madrid clashes and who was going to win the Cup and stuff like that, he'd talk about death. Why? Well, he said it helped him with his important project; a painting he called 'Speck of Dust on the Breeze'.
    This death thing was kind of creepy in a way. Each morning we'd meet for breakfast and he'd sit at a table – never at the bar - with his legs crossed at the knees, elegantly sipping his *café con leche* like some old-time movie star. He'd scour the newspapers for stories of death: road crashes, rail crashes, disasters, tragedies, anything and everything. He seemed convinced that in some way all the people concerned wanted to die, to end their own lives. You must know he was a big fan of the idea that we create our own life experience, and we have to take responsibility for everything that happens to us. I know he spent some time in India so I suppose that's where he picked up those ideas.
    An odd thing I remember is that he once told me he couldn't sleep without the light on. He had a fear of the dark, he said, which was a bit strange considering he always wore shades. I

didn't know he had problems with his sight though, until you mentioned it. I'm no psychologist, but I think he was full of guilt. You know what I mean?

He had a silly sense of humour, childish, you know? One of his favourites things was to say to Milagros, our breakfast girl, when she brought his morning coffee and *cruasán*, "And how are the alligator sandwiches today, *señorita*?" "*Muy, muy buenos*," she'd reply, knowing the script by heart. "That's good," he'd say, "then bring me one and make it snappy." You know, the old joke.

He hardly ever spoke about his family or his background. I did know he had a brute of an Irish father and a good-looking Italian mother, though. Mornings in the bar he tended to keep his eyes down or his shades on and just draw, doodle really, rarely looking at anyone direct, like he was ashamed or shy. I once asked if he'd ever been married or had any children, stuff like that; but he didn't answer. It seemed he hadn't heard me so I repeated it; but he just kept on scribbling and doodling in that damned notebook of his. Then, after a full two minutes of ignoring me and without a word, he just got up and walked out. Put his pencil in his shirt pocket where he always kept it, closed his notebook, put that in his jeans back pocket and walked straight out the door. It was weird, but controlled too like he was on a stage and acting out a part. I was left sitting there at the table feeling really stupid and with my mouth wide open, wondering what to do. Should I go after him and apologize? But what for, exactly? Am I glad I didn't because next morning there he was in his usual place, doodling away, shades round his eyes. He just looked up and smiled and said, 'Buenos días, Dan,' in that gentle way of his. So cool; I just loved the guy.

What else did he say? Well, sometimes he'd talk about the games people play; games between friends, between families and lovers. You remember what a good-looking man he was? Real chiselled jaw with high cheekbones - a little effeminate for my taste - but those really cool sea-green eyes and steely hair hacked into a Samuel Beckett bottle-brush; he was something. He seemed completely unaware of the sideways glances he got too, from men and women. Yes, he had plenty of natural style, that guy; dramatic-looking, you know. Winter mornings he'd wear that long white silk scarf that he said he picked up from some thrift store in London. The way he'd wrap it around and with his shades on he looked like he was on his way to an audition or something! I found out later from his brother, Alex, that that scarf was the only thing of his father's that he'd taken after he'd dropped dead in the pub.

Jack always talked about 'affairs of the heart', as he called them, as if he was discussing something like cooking or taking a shower. I mean, it was like there was no emotion, no feeling there: like a block of wood. The only time I remember he showed anything like emotion was once, when he was scanning through the newspaper, he came across an article about a small child suffering in some way, I can't remember how exactly. But he kind of gasped and seemed to hold his breath while tears just poured down his face. I found it, you know, quite embarrassing so excused myself and went to the bathroom. When I got back he was all composed and smiling and back to normal. Yes, he did seem a bit strange sometimes, that's a fact.

Apart from our rants about football and stuff, which to be honest was a big surprise as he didn't seem the kind of guy who'd be interested in anything so physical, he sometimes mentioned a woman in Madrid. Off he'd go Friday mornings regular as clockwork to see you, Miss Vanessa Buchanan-Tree. I used to say, 'She's gotta be worth it. Nobody could make up a name like that!' He never let on why he travelled all that way every week to see you but I had my suspicions. Just goes to show how wrong you can be.

He'd hinted that he hadn't had much of a childhood, and I knew he'd travelled around India living some kind of hippy existence contemplating his navel or something, but apart from that I thought what you saw was what you got with Jack. Mind you, I've never been one to ask questions. Live and let live, I say. Thankfully he never asked me much about my background either! But he did sometimes talk about painting, his latest work and his sources of inspiration, that kind of stuff. I'm sure he never sold anything back then, but that could have had more than a little to do with the fact that he never showed anyone what he'd done.

I often wondered where the money came from to go to Madrid and back each week, not to mention 'Miss Tree's fees'! I assumed he had a little tucked away somewhere. He mentioned a brother or two but to be honest I can't really recall anything in particular. He was pretty cagey. So, in a way, when I heard what had happened, what he'd done, it wasn't the biggest surprise. But it was still a shock because I liked him a lot; and I realised I'd never really known the guy.

I'd turned up as usual for my *café americano* and pork-fat *cruasán* and, seeing his chair empty and thinking he was probably in the bathroom, went outside to the ONCE booth to buy our weekly lottery ticket. We hardly ever won but we always expected the big prize and endlessly discussed how we'd spend it! When I came back his chair was still empty, and as Milagros put my breakfast in front of me, she said, "*Lo siento, cariño*, so sorry about your friend. I'm gonna to miss him," and turned and waddled back to the bar. Sweet, dumpy Milagros. Her main claims to fame were, one, her ability to pick up the raunchiest words and sentences from any tourist that came by; two, sashaying that ass around the tables and among the customers practising her bits and bites with a cigarette in one hand and a damp cloth in the other; and three, the size of her breasts, which somehow always threatened to escape from the confines of her skin-tight low-cut tee. I shouldn't be saying it, but Milagros was a dish in many senses of the word and in class I'd often daydream of taking her up on her offer of a little siesta. If it wasn't for the overpowering aroma of stale cigarettes and unwashed armpits, I might just have given in and fallen into her big bed. But the real miracle of her name seemed to come from her ability to be all things to all people at all times; ever-smiling and joking and returning lewd comments (mine included, I admit) about her overly hourglass figure, with responses that shocked tourists and her boss alike.

'What's that?' I shouted, jumping up after her. 'What about my friend? What's happened?' She was already serving another customer, pouring steaming milk into a large cup of coffee.

'Oh, they find his body early this morning, *cariño*, it hanging from *una viga* in his room for two days. You don't know, *cariño? Ay ay ay. ¡Que desastre!*' She looked at me with genuine sorrow, I could tell, even as she stuffed a huge pastry into her mouth. 'I'm glad it wasn't me that find him,' she continued, shuddering. 'They say me that the downstairs neighbour hear a crash, like a piece of furniture. But, you know, it was Navidad that day, so she wait til this morning to go up the stair to check what happen. When she get no answer she call to the *Guardia* and they kick the door down; too late though. *¡Que pena!* What a pity. Nice man, I'm gonna miss him. *Muy extraño*, but nice, you know? *Y ¡que guapo! Madre mía.* What eyes! *¡Hola, cariño! Buenos días,*" she shouted at a tourist with a map and a baseball cap, "and what can I do you for, big boy?"

So I ran all the way to the corner building where he lived in Plaza Mayor near those crazy zigzaggy steps – you know? - the ones that inspired Hemingway and Orson Welles?- and saw the police car outside. I dragged open the wooden door and skidded right across the tiled foyer. Taking the stairs three at a time I reached his *'atico'* to find the door open and a policeman and an expensively-dressed man inside – he looked like an older, fatter version of Jack. I blurted out, "What happened? Tell me! Jack was my friend!" The man put his arm around me and handed me a white cotton handkerchief. He introduced himself as Alex, Jack's brother.

We stood there, kind of sobbing for what seemed the longest time. Then eventually the policeman left and Alex told me how the neighbour had heard a thump like a piece of furniture falling over but did nothing as it was Christmas Day. Then, when she did remember to call the station, they sent a policeman who came and broke down the door. And there was Jack, hanging from the big central beam in his studio. Around his neck was that long, white silk scarf he'd wear on cold mornings; the only thing left from his rotten life in England, he'd said; from his old life of misery, which he'd only hinted at in our conversations.

Alex told me Jack had always blamed himself for the death of their eldest brother Charles who, as you know, seven years earlier had flung himself from the Paris rooftop of a building of yet another publisher who'd rubbished his work. Charlie had been the first of the brothers to break away from the family, travelling the world as a merchant seaman before settling in Paris. He'd been a writer all his life though, trying to get published but never making the grade. His poems and stories were not what people wanted at that time. Too dark, he was told, and too disjointed for any decent publisher to pick up on. Nowadays, of course, they'd be selling like hotcakes, but then it was a different market and poor Charlie really suffered for his art, Alex said. He and his wife Anna had no money and wouldn't take handouts from anyone in the family either. Charlie hit the bottle, big time, and refused to get any kind of job: nothing meaningful, just something to help them live a decent life. Whenever Alex was in Paris visiting a client or whatever, he'd stop off at the supermarket and get a bag of food and leave it outside Charlie and Anna's door.

But then, after Anna left him, Charlie turned into a recluse and refused to see anyone, least of all Alex. But his hatred, his venom, was all for Jack who, I'm sure, had never done anything to harm him. In fact, Jack adored Charlie; he was like a hero when they were young. In the past, he said, they even looked similar, both being tall, dark and damned good-looking. 'I often felt left out', Alex said, 'and jealous of their love-hate relationship.' Anyway, when Charlie died Jack fell apart and probably never really recovered.

Alex hadn't seen Jack since Charlie's funeral and was told by neighbours that he was always acting oddly. He had no obvious friends and, apart from going out each morning for breakfast, slept all day and worked all night. 'As you can see, Dan', Alex said, 'his output was prolific; but before today I had no idea the quality or quantity of his work.'

Well, Vanessa, I wiped my eyes and looked around the high-ceilinged room and saw dozens of canvases and frames leaning against the walls. More were stacked on shelves that were arranged around the small studio. I'd never seen anything like it; kind of like an art warehouse there were so many. And the room was all white: walls, ceiling, even the floor had been painted white. It was tidy too, as if nobody lived there. No real signs of life at all, like it was only used as a studio and then tidied up at the end of the day before going home.

So Alex and I peeled back one or two canvasses from the outer stack and held them up to look at them. I didn't know what to expect but I nearly fell flat on my face. They were extraordinary: full of light and life, and children. Children everywhere: children playing, laughing, riding horses, even flying through the air! He had painted enormous palm trees and grimacing statues, running policemen surrounded by swirls of thick red colour, walled gardens, a ruined arch, whispering animals and endless, endless pathways. What exquisite details and extraordinary colour combinations. It was like some crazy, psychedelic garden; he must have been permanently tripping! Alex and I spent about an hour in virtual silence just picking them through and holding them up to the light. He said that, of course they'd have to be catalogued and stored until he could decide what to do with them; being an art dealer he knew important people in the art world who'd be able to advise him.

As I seemed to be Jack's only real friend, he wanted me to take one, any picture I liked, as a gift in thanks and appreciation of my friendship with his brother. And, of course, the only other thing the Guardia found, on the floor near the elephant stool, was Jack's poem, handwritten in English on a piece of paper torn from a lined A4 pad. He probably shouldn't have done it, but as he couldn't understand English, he handed the poem to Alex and me. I believe Alex sent you a copy back then but, if not, I'm enclosing one now.

So there you'll all be, Vanessa, at Jack's big day in London. I'm sorry I won't be able to make it but we've just had another child, our 5th (a boy this time - guess what we're going to call him!) and Rosa isn't up to much travelling at the moment. I expect there'll be quite a turnout from the international art crowd though. Now, of course, everyone says how well they knew Jack and that he was their best buddy. And your Aunt Isabella will be there; have you met her yet? Alex will be there too, of course. He still keeps in touch from time to time to let me know how the paintings are doing, which galleries they're in, etc.

It's been ten years since I lost my mysterious friend, but over time Alex has filled me in on some of the details of their childhood. I wish I'd had the maturity and wisdom to read between the lines of what Jack hinted at during our breakfasts. I always felt though, it's none of my business, if he wants to talk, he'll talk; he knows I'm a friend and I'll listen. But perhaps he thought I'd judge him. Is that why he didn't confide in me? I'll never know. But thank God he had you to talk to, Vanessa.

So, anyway, after stashing 'Speck of Dust on the Breeze' under our bed for a couple of years - because to be honest it upset me too much even to think of it - when Rosa gave birth to our first, we decided to hang the picture on the big wall facing the balcony. After taking down everything else around that could distract from it, we set up dimmers and spotlights and stuff, like they do in the galleries. Like that, it seems that every time we look at it something fresh jumps out and reveals itself.

You know, sometimes I wake in the middle of the night with a sense that Jack's around, right there in the apartment, sometimes even in the girls' room. But that's OK, he was a cool guy, he'd never hurt them. So I just get up and open a beer and sit and gaze at the painting. Sometimes I'm still there when the sun comes up, just imagining Jack floating peacefully and silently through space.

2.
Three Point Turn
- London and Paris -

Vanilla Sunday
London, 1959

When Anna Devlin was tiny, her father would take her to an Italian ice-cream parlour for a once-a-month treat on Sundays. Her mother, Amelia, would shoo them out of the house so she could put her feet up and read the Sunday papers in peace and, truth to tell, enjoy a little after-lunch nap. Up till then in post-war England, the only kind of commercially available ice-cream had been a white slab of some unknown substance, suspiciously resembling pork fat, called Wall's Ice Cream.. Although it purported to be flavoured with vanilla it was virtually tasteless, but being ice-cold and pure white it was acceptable and considered exotic enough for the majority of people: a small slab of mystery. It was many years before Anna discovered the true taste of vanilla, the sensual, comforting quality of that spice pod from the East. She wondered, since, how such a misleading misnomer as 'vanilla ice-cream' could have been printed on the packaging, as there appeared to be no vanilla in it and even less cream.

The ice-cream parlour of Anna's childhood was called Fusciardi's. It was run by second generation Italians whose parents had emigrated from Casalattico in southern Italy in the early 1900s. Their intention was to escape the poverty of their background and offer a better future to their children.

Anna and her father would enter the *gelateria*, Arnold wearing his Sunday best dark brown suit with fine chalk stripe and Anna with a patriotic red, white and blue ribbon fluttering in her hair. After mock-formally greeting the plump middle-aged owner, Mariano, they would perch themselves on high vivid-pink and blue padded plastic chairs – the '50s equivalent of psychedelia – at a small pistachio-green round table. Anna's short legs would dangle and kick wildly, unable to reach the black-and-white checked linoleum floor.

The ice-cream was divine, they both agreed, nodding; beyond description. Delicate, long-necked metal spoons would be plunged into thick glass containers. Scoops of mango, strawberry and orange ice-cream extracted, sometimes dripping with melted chocolate that miraculously stayed soft no matter how long it had covered the freezing ice-cream, which was never long.

Anna and Arnold had a ritual. First they would taste a little of their own ice-cream, then they would pause and lick their lips dramatically, then offer their sundae to the other to taste. They would smile questioningly with a faraway look in their eyes, lick their lips again and say, *'Mmmm, questo gelati è squisito!'* as Mariano had tried to teach them. Anna would elongate the vowel until it became 'squeeeezito', savouring the feel of the word with an exaggerated smile until Mariano could no longer hold in his laughter at their antics. It was an entertainment, he wistfully told his wife who worked faithfully in the back room mixing the ingredients. What a pair they were; the man who so truly adored his daughter that he could have been Italian and the doll-like charmer who had a toothy smile for everyone. Mariano was envious, having never been favoured with the longed-for child.

When Anna and Arnold could no more scrape and excavate even the tiniest sliver of ice-cream from their glass tubs, they would put down their spoons with a flourish (pinkie fingers aloft), delicately dab at the corners of their mouths with the flimsy pink tissues conveniently placed on the table for this purpose and smile broadly. Anna would whisper shyly, 'Thank you Mariano - *delizioso.*' Mariano, beaming with pride, would then present the bill to Arnold who, after tipping generously, would push back his chair, stand up and walk around the table to Anna.

With a flamboyant gesture he would take hold of the back of her chair and pull it gently away from the table as she jumped noisily down onto the floor. Then, with chins up and heads high they would glide towards the door, which Mariano was happy to hold open for them, and cry dramatically, '*Grazie, Mariano, arrivederci!*'. Out they would walk, arm in arm, straight-backed and elegant, Anna's short legs stretching out to match her father's stride, while his shortened considerably to match hers. They were quite a pair.

It was many years later, at her husband Charles' funeral in Paris, that Anna discovered that Mariano, the owner of her childhood *gelateria,* had in fact been the only nephew of Charles' grandfather, Gaetano Fusciardi.

Daddy Loves You
London, 1982

"Yes, hello?"

Anna! It's me. Dad."

"Oh. Hello."

"How are you, sweetheart? Hey! Glad I've caught you in at last. Every time I ring I just seem to get that bloody answer machine. I hate it! It just feels so strange, I don't know, it makes me feel stupid. Never know what to say. But anyway, it's good to hear your voice at last – 'live on air' as they say! Ha ha! Anna? Are you there? Hello?'

"Yes, I'm here. What do you want?"

"Well, I just said. Find out how you are – you know – and to see you. Anna, look, I'm sorry I missed your birthday – is it 25 or 26 now? Well, I'm in town and thought we could have a spot of lunch to celebrate it – just the two of us. Me and my Annie, like old times. You know? Thought we could go to that place that you used to like along the road from the house. Those Greek Cypriots ran it. What was their name - Philipot – Philipou? Maybe it's not there any more. It was called..... The Stockpot! That's it! They used to do those special lunchtime menus. Not bad and quite cheap if I remember. What do you say? Shall we give it a whirl?"

"I can't. Sorry. I'm meeting Mother today. I always meet her on Fridays. We go shopping and have lunch together afterwards. What do you want to see me for anyway?"

"Nothing special. Well, I just told you – your birthday. I'm in town and I thought I'd see if you were free. Do I need a reason to see my daughter? When did I ever need a reason to see you, sweetheart?"

"Well, you don't bother to see me very often, that's all. I can't remember the last time you called and invited me to lunch."

"Hey, that's not fair. You know how difficult it is for me nowadays, what with the shop and all. Besides, you never want to see me anyway. You always say – I can't... I'm busy – like you'd rather be doing anything than spending time with your poor old dad. What have I done to deserve this kind of treatment, that's what I'd like to know.

"Anna? You there?"

"Yes. I'm here."

"Huh! You always were a bit spoilt. Your bloody mother's fault. Never appreciated anything I tried to do for you both. Bloody woman. All she ever did was whinge on about how she'd 'married down'. Never went short of a bit of food on the table, though, did she?"

"Oh, here we go. You walked out the door when I was six. No word, no goodbye, nothing. How could you do that without even a goodbye? Didn't it occur to you how much I might suffer after you left? But you're always full of excuses. Never any different, even after all this time. Why don't you just leave me alone? You only ever wanted me for one thing anyway. In fact, you only ever call now when you want something."

"What? How dare you! How dare you speak to me like that, miss. Look, I don't have to bother, you know. I've got plenty of lady friends I could take to lunch if I wanted to. Plenty."

"Lady friends? Listen, I'm not one of your lady friends. I'm your daughter, in case you'd forgotten. Don't you know the difference yet? What poor Mother had to put up with. No wonder she's batty as hell. I swear, one of these days I'm going to tell her all about you.

"And how dare I? How dare you even dare to pick up the phone and... 'just going to see if my Annie's in and wants to come to lunch with her old dad'... Well, she doesn't. And she doesn't want you to phone her again. OK? So just leave me alone. I didn't need you then and for sure I don't need you now.

"Just leave me alone."

click

"Hello, Anna? It's me again sweetheart. I might have known you'd switch that damned machine on. You know how much I hate it. Look, I don't want an argument. Fact is I need to talk to you about something. It's quite – well in fact I'm a bit frightened to be honest. I've been having some problems with the old heart recently – nothing too serious – don't get worried - but I'm a bit concerned, you know? Actually, I've got to go in and have an op – some kind of bypass they call it – next week in fact. All this talk about waiting lists, but they get you in quick if they want to. They said if I don't have this done straight away – well, they're always scaremongering, aren't they? Makes them feel important I suppose. So I'll have to close up the shop for a few weeks - can't trust any of the staff these days. Turn your back for five minutes and everything disappears. God knows what they'd get up to if I wasn't there to watch them. They're such a thieving bunch - I had to sack one of them the other day. Caught him red-handed walking out with half a lamb under his arm. Between you and me, Anna, I'm thinking of closing up for good and moving up north. You know, stay with your Aunt Lizzie for a bit. Try something else, something easier; butchering's not what is was. I don't know - I'm getting too old for all this. A bit of gardening would be nice – plants and flowers – some peace and quiet for a change."

   beep

   "As I was saying, Anna, things aren't what they were. I can hardly make ends meet these days. Whole damn world's gone vegetarian, that's the trouble. It was you that started that all those years ago. You and your hippy friends. Thing is - as I said - I'm a bit scared and I've got no-one to come with me or anything when I go in. And I just wondered – if you could – you know – come along and kind of 'hold my hand' a bit. I feel daft asking you like this but there's no-one else and I feel a bit scared, you know? Actually, truth is I'm terrified. I have a kind of premonition that something could be really wrong and they might not be able to put it right. Silly of me, I know, but - well you know."

   beep

   "It's me again, Anna. Look, please just come to the hospital with me, just this once. You don't have to stay long. Try and forget the past and help your old dad, just this once. I always loved you – you know that. You were always my pretty girl. Like a little doll, you were. Please call me back, Anna."

click

"Anna? I said I'm sorry. Forgive me. Can you do that? I need you very much now. Your old dad really needs you, Anna. Look, call me back. I'm at the flat. If I don't hear from you, I'll try again tomorrow.

"OK, sweetheart? Daddy loves you!"

click

Six/Twenty Six
London, 1982

Anna sat without making a sound. Her father lay on the bed before her, his chest rising and falling; his breathing laboured, agonized and slow. She watched him now as once before long ago, with a sense of not knowing if she would see him again. She studied his large hands – butcher's hands - so capable of inflicting pain upon others; but for her only tenderness and caresses. The only thing she could do now was to hold them tightly, her fingertips exploring the bones and knuckles, the wrinkles of skin. She smoothed his fingernails and wondered what he was thinking as she gazed into his face.

Arnold sensed she was watching him, acknowledging that this time he was leaving and not returning ever. As once before, he knew there would be no going back. Even though her mother had written him about how Anna had cried for weeks, curled up in bed, confused but unable to express such devastation in her six-year-old life. Again he was moving on not daring to allow himself to think even a little about her, or of his grief and guilty pain.

His flickering eyes travelled round the room and rested on Anna's anxious face. Suddenly, quite unexpectedly, the love and tenderness that only a father could feel for his child welled up inside him; never before expressed, pushed down until it had become cold and heavy. The fear of loving, but now losing again, his only daughter became too much for him and he gathered all his strength and roared like a bull. Pictures flashed through his mind. He tried hard to stop them but everything was shifting out of control: a chain of images threaded together with pain.

"But the good times?" his weary voice groaned. "Surely there were some?" Then, before he realised what was happening, peace enveloped him and he glided forward.

Still clasping one hand, Anna shaded her eyes from the brightness as sounds of the seaside came thick and fast; squealing children being warned to 'be careful' and 'not go in too far'; seagulls screaming overhead. She could smell the salt in the air. Happy days: hungry sun-kissed bodies exhausted from play and another day tomorrow promising the same. Arnold's large brown hands scooping her up and over his head, depositing her squarely across his shoulders. How she adored him! She threw back her head and laughed clinging to fistfuls of hair; weaving her fingers through the length of it, the fiercer to hold on to him.

Anna opened her eyes and stroked his hair now, tenderly as she would a child's; realising the whole thing had ended but needing to keep him with her just a little longer. How still the room seemed, sterile and bare. The vase of get-well flowers received that morning with a weak smile now pushed aside; forgotten. A sense of 'this is all there is' hung in the air. Anna closed her eyes.

10th September '97
Knightsbridge, London, 1997

Hello Anna

It's been *such* a long time since you called – I sometimes think you've forgotten me! I know how busy you are with the animals - your 'children' – so I'm putting pen to paper myself. I had the strangest dream last night - we were back in India again. Do you remember how magical it was? We stepped off the plane and felt reborn. There was something 'sublime' in the air you said - you loved that word! But there *was* an intangible quality, a sense of wonder. I remember we both wrote in our journals that we would 'keep ourselves fully open to possibility' and that we 'felt more connected to higher energies than ever before'. How pompous! Did we really say those things darling? I rather think you brought out the hippie in me.

I don't think I ever told you how thrilled I was when you invited me to go with you, because we'd never been very close. Nowadays of course they'd say I never 'bonded' with you when you were born – that horrid, modern way of saying something that frightened me more than you could imagine. I thought I knew what would be waiting for me when I took you home to Daddy, but as it turned out he adored you and spent more time with you than I expected. Well, darling, you were *so* beautiful. "My little Princess," he'd say. "The prettiest girl in the world." In truth I was a little jealous of all the time he spent with you, especially when the first thing he'd do when he got home was to kiss you goodnight and just ignore me! And with me sitting there all evening waiting for him too. Beastly man! He wanted to do everything for you, things that were my job, things that a man shouldn't get himself involved in, I say. I sometimes wondered if he was up to something. But anyway, that's all in the past now. Let's forget all that. I expect you've got no idea what I'm talking about. Best really.

Back to India! Thankfully you had no trouble with your poor legs but I remember we did have to fend off several admirers who saw two attractive women on their own as fair game. Darling, those dark-skinned 'don juans' went to such ingenious lengths, didn't they! Remember that piano-player in Delhi who disconnected your phone and switched off the hotel fuse-boxes plunging us all into darkness? He hammered on your door shouting "Fire! Fire! This is the manager - open the door immediately and come out as you are!" Thank goodness you had the presence of mind to get dressed first even though the hotel was apparently burning down around our ears! What a night that was, with the police and all! I'm sure the other guests didn't believe you. To be honest, I wasn't sure if I did at the time. In fact, I had rather thought it was me he liked.

Do you remember that old yogi at the side of the road? As usual you had no problem charming him into posing for that wonderful photograph - you've always had a way with men. Darling, I have a little confession to make. There was a competition running in the local newspaper a few years back for unusual snaps and things and I sent that photo in. I had to put it under my name of course. Actually darling, the exercise bike I gave you the last Christmas you were over – I knew how much you needed it to strengthen your legs - and I did feel a little guilty at winning so much money since that good-for-nothing husband of yours left you with such debts. (By the way, what happened to that bike? Did you take it with you on the boat? I would have had it if I'd known you didn't want it any more).

Do you remember that 'official' hotel palm-reader? Well! He thought he was the 'bees' knees' all right. Quite 'pressed and polished' wasn't he, considering he was just a servant. I'll never forget how loudly he announced (mostly I think for the benefit of the other guests who were pretending not to listen) that one day you would have three husbands, eight children and be 'as rich a Maharani'! How wrong could he be darling – you hadn't even caught one husband yet! And that dirty smelly fortune-teller at the roadside café - do you remember how he kept trying to cover the holes in his trousers? At least he wouldn't take any money. What was it he said he saw? Oh yes, a large black bat, fire and destruction! He could have been talking about the car accident I suppose. He wanted you to have another coffee, so he could read at least a little happiness in your coffee grouts; but you wouldn't. I thought that was rather mean of you, darling, since I needed to see something bright for you too. I always wondered, when you went back to collect your scarf from the table, did you actually give him some money? I did ask you not to – it does so upset the balance of the economy in these places.

Darling, we saw some frightful sights didn't we. Delhi Station at six in the morning – remember? - all those smelly men blocking our way to the train. We very nearly missed it because of them. Just lying there on the ground like spoons - all night by the look of it – hundreds of them. Thank goodness that policeman came and blew his whistle when he did - that made them jump! If he hadn't we'd have been completely stranded.   But darling, the fun of boiled eggs, curried potatoes, and lukewarm tea from those little flasks for breakfast! Really, they did try, didn't they? Sweet people.

You know, darling, in India you seemed to discover a peace and calm that I'd never seen in you before, an inner tranquillity in a way. You often said you'd been guided to that place of extremes – 'grinding poverty and sumptuous wealth,' you said. Talking of which, what fabulous hotels we stayed in; 'All converted Maharaja's palaces,' it said in the guidebook. But my god, the filthy rat-infested streets, and right next to those gorgeous gardens too. I'm surprised it was allowed. And the animals, 'both revered and reviled' – what a strange state of affairs that was. Remember those big white cows that even had right-of-way over the traffic as they roamed about the streets causing utter chaos? And those dancing monkeys, beaten and poked at with sticks? Though they were quite harmless because their teeth had been wrenched from their poor little mouths when they were young. That really upset you.

I remember you said a strange thing, darling, that in India you learned acceptance; that there is no right or wrong, good or bad – there just 'is'. I sometimes think about that nowadays and wonder what you meant. Before we set off you waffled on that you'd been reading about cause and effect and reincarnation and such. About how these people lived by just accepting their situation, sure in the knowledge that 'next time round' as with 'last time round' things would be different. What on earth were you talking about? You really were just too deep for me sometimes. But maybe in some way India did made sense of your accident, darling. Is that what you meant?

Anna, you probably won't remember, but when you were tiny you had some strange sickness that led to pneumonia, and it left you with a kind of asthma that laid you up regularly until you were six - when Daddy left in fact. The doctors didn't have a clue what to do with you and couldn't understand your sadness. You became very withdrawn too. Anyway, after one of your 'turns' Daddy gave you a jigsaw puzzle of the Taj Mahal, which you did until the edges wore away. You loved it so much and often said that one day you'd see it for real and that would make everything better. When we did see it, in that first moment framed through the window of the temple, what happened to you? You just collapsed. What was it that touched you so deeply darling? I wish I knew. Was it a memory from when you were little? Remember how the colour of the stone changed from soft pink to deep rose as the sun moved around it? You said the water was the colour of pomegranates. It was so beautiful - and the white marble seemed to shimmer in the sun. I don't know what it was, but something affected you badly, and you couldn't even stop crying when that rather gorgeous man offered to take our photo – I was cross. I do remember how electric the air felt; the birds were singing and people were whispering as if they were in a sacred place. Darling, if only we could speak together sometimes you might be able to tell me what was wrong then, what was going on in your mind. But after all this time, I suppose it's not important now.

In your life, you've travelled to some beautiful places – I've always envied you that - and seen many breathtaking sights, but after India you were never the same again – you said you could never be free of the East. Is that why you upped and left us all darling, after Charles died? I do wish I knew.

Anyway, that was about my dream. I hope you think of me often. I miss you, you know. A phone call when you get a moment in your busy life wouldn't go amiss. The library has said it will set me up with 'a digital address' whatever that is - some new Government service for us oldies, I suppose. They seem to think it'll help us keep in touch, but then they don't know you, do they Anna?

I'm quite well really, under the circumstances. Doctor Mac tells me I'm as strong as an ox and I'll live to be a hundred. He must know something I don't!

A big kiss to you and the 'little ones'. Hope to hear something from you soon.

Your loving Mother

Charles
Paris, 1990

My dearest Anna

It was never my intention to leave you remembering the worst of me. I know it's unforgivable to leave you with my debts, my long-ago-forgotten ambition, my drinking, my depressive shadows, my anger, my crassness.

My dearest wish was always to leave you my eloquence, my joy like bright shining jewels careening elegantly across the page like pearls studding your velvet throat and the milky lobes of your ears. The best of me would have been to give you inky Parisian nights, one palm touching the other's soft palm as we inched our way along the Seine, whispering out our dreams and hearing them come back like sighs on the breeze.

My offer once, long ago, was my love for you and what I believed was my talent. That and my soul, an untouched wisp of smoke the purpose of which is a mystery except when we sleep or die. What else could I offer you but my hopes and dreams, those ephemeral twin deceivers forever to be joined at the hip of cliché? But my gems no longer sparkle, dearest Anna, they just drop from my pen like lead weights, spoiling the perfection of a pristine page. They fight and argue and attack each other like members of a family that have never learned to live in harmony. My words damage each other as surely as the blows from my father's belt when I was a boy.

My dearest Anna, I want you to know beyond any doubt that you have been my guiding light, my refuge of sanity and peace, my beacon of light in a dark, dark world. I realise now that my desire to express myself through words on the page is an insult to the reader, my need to exorcise my ghosts an exercise in arrogance and self-deception. Anna, the last and only true gift I can give you now is your release from your commitment to me, and my gratitude for your belief in me. I will not put you through more hell. My deepest wish is that with another you will find the happiness you deserve and the children you long for. For sure you do not deserve my failure as a husband, companion, provider, lover, and friend.

Anna, you have been everything I could ever want in a wife. Your years of protective layers of loyalty, pulled on each day like a familiar coat; I hope they have never been taken for granted. With you my life has been comfortable and safe. I have given you nothing but pain and I can no longer do this.

Suicide is a life sentence for those who remain; their whole lives condemned. Please forgive me for this last act of selfishness.

Charles

3.
Beyond the Purple Bougainvillea
- Casalattico, Italy -

Garden of Dreams

Tucked up high behind wrought iron railings stands a house, its walls of patchy cream stone darkening with age, but hiding secrets far darker. Entering the house from the garden and up two steps there is a tall arched doorway, which leads to wide outer oak doors studded with hinged iron. Up two more steps and a porch-way carries you through towards smaller, more ornate doors; the bottom of timber and the top of such wildly-coloured glass that they say it caused a sensation when it arrived 200 years ago. Although the inner doors are usually kept closed, a sisal mat sits on the stone floor just inside the porch. A brass lamp hangs from the ceiling.

Outside again where to either side of the oak doors squat terracotta urns of oversized blue, pink and white hydrangeas, blousy and full. A sensuous driveway winds from the house towards double-gates set beneath a stone, arched frame, topped by pots tumbling out their petrified fruit. Black metal railings run in both directions from the gates, separating the garden and its mysteries from everyday life and the road beyond.

In the ancient garden grow trees of many shapes and textures: weeping willows, their branches catching on the wind and sweeping the ground like delicate feather fronds, cypresses, tall and proud and linked, they say, with Pluto the Roman god of the underworld. The trees provide not only good shade but a break from the flickering tail-end of the madness-inducing tramontano wind as it expires after its north-east trajectory. There are dense junipers, the berry-oil of which is still used to flavour gin, and the tough centre-stage Japanese pagoda tree which, in late summer and after 30 long years of growth, bears elongated panicles of tiny white pea-like flowers, fragrant and creamy. Everywhere is found pink and white jasmine, a single vine of which can perfume an entire garden, and fragrant honeysuckle with its flashy flowers attracting hummingbirds and butterflies throughout the summer. Gnarled branches of wisteria twine around stone columns that support an ancient pergola, dressed in late spring with delicate mauve blossoms and providing necessary shade in the height of summer.

Old stone steps, gravel paths and foliage contribute to the appeal of this wondrous place; a waterfall cascades past pink bougainvillea which hover over still, white water-lilies basking in the cool of a pond. Rustic pots of colourful petunias enliven the simple stone wall that surrounds the pond; leopard plants, rounded and sculptured by nature's own hand, echo the swelling forms of antique oil jars. The blossom and fruit of meticulously pruned lemon trees in hundred year old terracotta pots give out not only intense, delightful fragrance, but add colour and ornament to the scene. Throughout the year purple bougainvillea bushes flower, their abundance of dazzling bracts still delighting the eye on wintry Casalattico mornings.

This garden of dreams was an enchanted place to hide, or lose oneself, when the pain of daily life became too much to bear for Pasqualina.

Memories

Inside the garden, multi-coloured kittens would dash helter-skelter the length of the railings, while the patriarchal and dominant ginger patrolled the perimeter wall. Throughout the day, locals passing by would stop to gaze into the garden. Governesses, marching small children to school and weighed down with bags of daily requirements, would take advantage of precious moments to rest their eyes upon the lush scene beyond the railings, while their charges got distracted by the scampering of the kittens. Elderly couples out for a morning stroll would hold hands as firmly as they did during courtship and stand and smile absent-mindedly while gazing into the garden, a far-way look in their eyes.

As a young man, Alfonso was employed at the big house as a full-time gardener. He knew he was lucky to have the job as it was common knowledge around that he was 'spooked', that he had possessed strange powers since he was born. Unable to get much work in the years since he was fired, he barely survived and became heavy with bitterness. When his wife died, his unmarried daughter, Maria, dutifully took care of him. Still resentful of the disgrace his dismissal brought to the family, she realised he was outwardly angry but inwardly pleased that she did not have what was needed to hook and hold on to an important man from the city. Father and daughter rarely spoke, but their common love of animals and plants continued to unite them.

Most evenings, about an hour before sunset, as the Casalattico sky turned to deep russet, Pasqualina would bid farewell to her guests after walking them to the large wrought-iron gates at the end of the drive. A small, fragile woman with high cheekbones, cloudy brown eyes and fine white hair pulled back elegantly into a bun, she had been living in the house since she was born there 85 years before. Luigi, her long-dead husband, Il Signor, bred the white-coated Maremma sheepdogs that had been used in Italy for centuries. During their unhappy marriage he routinely cheated on Pasqualina, frequently hit her and often ignored her completely. He also sent her three young boys away to Ireland and she never saw them again until they were men.

Pasqualina would sit in her garden, close to the bougainvillea, chatting with friends and family round an ornately carved table brought across from Morocco, unaware of the locals who studied her from the railings that separated her private domain from the outside world. While giving the impression of listening to and hanging on her guests' every word, smiling and making the politest sounds of encouragement, her eyes would wander to the purple bushes. For 60 years La Signora struggled with her memories while guarding a terrible secret.

Leonardo

Leonardo never forgot the moment he first set eyes on Pasqualina. He was barely 20 and she five years older and married to the master for only six months. There were rumours that there had been some difficulty in finding her a decent husband due to her wilful nature and mature years, but some kind of financial deal must have been struck between Luigi and her father for he was well known for his meanness. As if to make up for her husband's lack of affection, Leonardo worshipped her and would have done anything to marry her himself and make a life together, given the chance. It was her sense of fun he adored, her ability to laugh at the silliest things including, behind his back, her husband.

Life's a shit, Leonardo would think while secretly driving himself crazy watching Pasqualina out of the corner of his eye; her sensuous way of slowly tossing her head and letting her smoky-brown eyes gaze from beneath that wonderful corn-coloured hair. She could get angry though and the source of her fury was always her husband, who delighted in teasing and taunting his new bride, just to see her react and get mad. But Leonardo knew you had to be a fool to believe that Il Signor and his feisty wife didn't end up in the big bedroom at the far end of the house after a screaming match. He would go outside and walk down the narrow, cobbled path to the cages, light a cigarette and try to erase the vision of husband and wife. It was obvious to everyone who worked for Il Signor that Leonardo fell in love with Pasqualina the first moment he saw her, and he knew instinctively that she felt more than a mild attraction for him.

Whenever Luigi was around, Pasqualina and Leonardo would avoid eye contact and she would speak to him sharply in words of one syllable. She let it be known that she had no thoughts for him other than one would for any kennel worker in her husband's employ.   But when they were alone she would smile openly and giggle, and flash her eyes in that way women do when they know they are being appraised. Leonardo started working for Luigi as a young man and then he fell for Pasqualina, but as the years went by he never married and always carried a flame for her.

His job, starting at 6.30 am each day, was to clean and wash out the 20 cages after moving the dogs out to the exercise yard one at a time for their morning run. Pasqualina would hear him laughing, cursing and shouting at the dogs as he worked. His despair and frustration over La Signora was so great that occasionally he would kick out at them in anger if they did not move fast enough. He believed the dogs knew he cared for them though, for they willingly returned to him when it was time to be led back to their cages.

Pasqualina

Pasqualina had grown up in Casalattico; a town with big houses and a tiny school half a kilometre away. Her parents had encouraged her to study as they believed it was necessary to be more than just a pretty face to catch a good husband. She and her five brothers had all attended the same daily class in the schoolroom presided over by the doughty Signora Morelli, freshly qualified from the prestigious 'Academy of Rome'.

On her 15th birthday, Pasqualina decided she had had enough of formal study and never went back to Signora Morelli's classroom again. Her youngest brother carried the handwritten letter to Signora informing her that Pasqualina would no longer be taking classes. Unfortunately no-one though to comment on it to her parents and it was six months before they discovered that she had been spending her days writing a diary and scribbling and drawing in her bedroom. Although her parents continued to pay for her place in the private school, by the time they discovered her secret life it was voiced that Pasqualina had been 'out of the system' for too long. In reality a deep embarrassment was felt all round for the lack of parental knowledge of what their children were up to, so they punished her accordingly by removing all her books and pens. It turned out that an educated, spirited, free-thinking young wife was not something that the majority of young Italian men of good stock thought worthy of having at their side, so it was to be another ten years before her disappointed father succeeded in walking her down the aisle.

One cold dark morning, six months after the night he and Pasqualina had finally taken advantage of Luigi being away in Rome, Leonardo realised all was not well. She carried her head lower than usual and he sensed she was trying to avoid his gaze. The other servants were not their usual chatty selves either, attending to their chores with studied detail and using exaggerated movements. Everyone in the house was quiet that morning and a strange energy hung in the air. Leonardo moved around the room, making jokes and trying to catch her eye. When he saw what at first looked like dirt on her face, an area as large as a man's hand stretching from beneath her jaw to above her eye, hidden and swollen like an overripe plum, he swallowed hard but said nothing. The workers were sitting round the kitchen table eating breakfast and a sharp glance from cook told them that Il Signor was approaching. A shiver of fear pulsed through the room. Leonardo noticed that Pasqualina's hands were shaking so much that she had to put down the bread knife she had been holding before she dropped it. Then, resting the heels of her wrists on the table-top, fingers curled upwards, she leaned forward on them swaying slightly, heavy and awkward. She started shaking as her husband lumbered into the room.

"You!" Luigi barked at Leonardo, stabbing a hard, bony finger at him. "Come with me. I need something moved."

Leonardo rose to his feet and followed, scraping back his heavy wooden chair and quietly placing his spoon on the table. He knew that the food would be stone cold when he got back but nobody dared ask the master to wait, not even for a second.

Two Angels

Pasqualina drifted in and out of consciousness, punches and kicks weakening her until she slipped out of her body and descended onto a soft, white cloud. This was familiar, it had happened many times before. Her angels had once again taken charge of the situation. What Pasqualina called 'observer-angel' had gently drawn her out of her physical body and handed her over to 'protector-angel' to take care of her for a while. How often they had had to stand back and watch Luigi humiliate his wife; invisibility rendering them helpless in the face of such bullying and brutality.

From her cushion of cloud, Pasqualina knew that her babies - Leonardo's babies? - were suffering more with each well-aimed boot and she sensed rather than felt them separate from their vital lifeline of tissue and blood.

The three souls that had been waiting for their opportunity to re-enter the world together detached from their mother and coolly resigned themselves to another interminable wait. The angels watched the silver cords dim and fade as incandescent fireflies of light shot off in different directions, leaving behind three small grey empty sacs. Before the angels left, they brushed their fingertips over Pasqualina's eyes allowing her a short restful sleep before the doctor arrived to shake her awake again.

Dr. Vella hated being called out once he had settled in for the night; worse still was if it happened after he had gone to bed and his wife had blown out the candle. He had already been called up to the big house twice that month. 'My god,' he thought. 'What is it with these people? More than two cups of gin and they lose all sense of propriety. Not only do good manners go straight out the window, but aggression and violence fly in.' He sighed and reached into his bag for the small vial of smelling salts. 'If I had a lira for every domestic incident from drinking too much gin....'

Alfonso's Curse

Each of the three bundles were tiny, no bigger than a week-old kitten. They were wrapped in white linen and placed side by side in the shallow grave under the largest bougainvillea bush. Alfonso looked at them for some time trying to figure out why on earth someone would bury cats in this way. Lord knew there were enough stray ones living and dying in the garden around the house but who would go to the trouble of wrapping them so carefully and placing them here? Or maybe, he thought, they were pups that had died at birth and Il Signor wanted to dispose of them without anyone knowing what had happened to them. Whatever, Alfonso sensed he should leave well alone but his curiosity got the better of him and, after glancing round quickly, he picked up the smallest bundle and unwrapped the cloth. He didn't hear Luigi coming up behind him until it was too late. "Hey, you! Stupid! What do you think you're doing? What are you up to?"

It was too late to put it back so Alfonso continued to hold the baby, its eyes and nose clogged tight with dried blood and mucus, black hair tightly matted and stuck to its head. He gazed at the dried, shrivelled form in his hand; it fitted perfectly. No-one moved, neither Alfonso kneeling on the ground nor Luigi, looming tall and large behind him.

"Trust you to find them. Always sticking your nose in where it's not wanted. Well you just keep your mouth shut and nobody will be any the wiser."

Alfonso could hardly breathe or drag his eyes from the tiny body with its arms raised, frozen forever in its gesture of surrender.

"Did you hear what I said?" shouted Luigi, growing angry. "Bastard! You just forget you've ever seen this and everything will be all right. You hear me?"

Alfonso slowly re-wrapped the tiny form and placed it back in its cold grave alongside the other two. He looked up at Il Signor with tears in his eyes.

"I can't forget this, Signor," he whispered. "How do you expect me to pretend I've never seen this?"

Luigi shrugged his shoulders and walked away but stopped and said over his shoulder, "You do what you like, but who's going to believe you? It would be your word against mine. So I suggest you forget what you've seen, keep your mouth shut, mind your own business and get back to work." At this Luigi strode off without looking back. "Arrogant bastard. How could La Signora live every day with that monster?"

With care he scooped back the earth and patted it down, cursing Il Signor under his breath. "He doesn't deserve all this – the house, La Signora. Bastard! He won't get away with it. I'll show him who's the boss here. He'll wish he hadn't spoken to me like that. A curse on him. He'll never be happy. Neither him nor anyone that bears his name." Alfonso's simple mind could hardly grasp what had happened; all he knew was he had to be careful. If word ever got out about what he'd found, he would lose his job and never get another like it.

"No wonder nothing grows here," he mused, as he walked back to the house.

4.
The Leather Coat
- London -

All Cool

"He divorced his wife for you, darling; the least you can do is marry him!"

Sofia tapped her pink cigarette against the side of the ashtray and noisily took another sip of Babycham. She licked her lips at the thought of a famous photographer becoming part of the family. Vanessa and Daniel Tree had met at the inauguration of Mr Chow in Knightsbridge, the first designer restaurant of 60s London. Daniel's snappy lime-green Mr Freedom fedora complemented the wide-lapelled cream suit he had bought that morning from Joseph of Molten Street. His shoes were of fine, red lizard-skin. Vanessa was in full Biba regalia: gold velvet pants-suit, thigh-high lace-up suede boots, matching deep purple feather boa and enough dark eye shadow to make a panda wince. Her best friend Jenny had nearly convinced her to rent an Afghan hound to take to the party but, attractive as the idea was as a fashion statement, Vanessa could not bear to exploit an animal. It had proved unnecessary to attempt to attract any attention, though, as she and Daniel had taken one look at each other, recognised a style soul-mate, and fallen instantly in lust.

Next morning a heavy gold ring fell from Daniel's pocket as he picked up his cream herringbone trousers. The night before, he had laid them neatly across the chair by the Regency Suite four-poster. The ring bounced twice and then rolled in an arc across the floor, clattering to a halt by Vanessa's right toe. It rocked briefly before balancing on the diamond full-stop to the wavy letter 'D'. Vanessa and Daniel both froze for enough time to allow him to compose his features into a look of non-surprise when she glanced up at him.

"Er... I did mention it in the taxi. Maybe you don't remember? You'd really had a lot to drink. But it's cool. It's not a problem. OK?"

He held her face in his hands and gently kissed her lips.

"Renée and I have an open marriage; she does what she wants and so do I. It works well. No hang-ups, no hassle. Free spirits. Capiche?"

He smiled down at her frowning face.

"Yeah," he continued, "she's totally cool about it. She knows there's no way I can be a 'one-woman guy', not with the opportunities that come my way when I'm working. In fact," he whispered, inching forward, "between you and me she says it makes it exciting. Sometimes she even begs me to bring someone famous home! You know, so we can have a party. Yeah, it's true - on my life! So I promise, it's not a problem. OK?" His fingertips brushed her skin.

Vanessa could not think of a single thing to say, other than, "OK.".

"OK." he whispered. "Come here."

Twins

It took Vanessa just six months to discover that he also had two small daughters. So she packed her enormous, yellow leather Gladstone bag, jumped into her silver Triumph Herald soft-top and roared off to Cornwall to forget him. And she tried hard; while Daniel was busily extricating himself from his marriage to Renée, a grubby-looking small-time model from somewhere in Wales, Vanessa did a stint as a 'Bluecoat' at Kingpins Holiday Camp, that 60s Mecca for the 'I've paid so bloody well entertain me' kind of holidaymaker. It seemed like a thousand people helped her celebrate her 21st birthday there but Vanessa got so drunk and felt so sorry for herself that she spent the next week in bed, depressed and mostly alone. Paper plates and cups littered the floor of her chalet and the fullness of the ashtrays gave her chalet-mate serious cause for concern.

"Damn," she thought. "I really do miss Daniel."

Six months later, when she realised he was serious about divorcing Renée, Vanessa wasted no time in getting back to London and installing herself in his fashionable Earls Court penthouse.

In London they lived happily 'in sin' for two years while Daniel's divorce was in process. As soon as the ink was dry on the decree, however, parental pressure for them to tie the knot was on. Within weeks, their wedding at Chelsea Town Hall was organised to be squeezed in after that of some vaguely recognisable American actress and her bodyguard. It was not long before their relationship started its descent, as Vanessa fought to overcome her increasing feelings of insecurity and Daniel his feelings of entrapment. Their normally happy German Shepherds, Trixie and Jojo, started snapping and snarling and getting on everyone's nerves. Even their river barge, 'Meg', their weekend pride and joy, developed an inexplicable list and had to be taken into dry dock for investigation.

The final nail in the coffin of their pre-nuptial bliss was when the heavy emotional guns came forward: Daniel's twin daughters Julie and Chrissie, whom he saw twice a month. They demanded to know all the plans.

"Dad, when you and Vanessa get married, will we be bridesmaids?"

"Well, you know, we're not sure we are getting married. Besides, Vanessa doesn't like church weddings. So if we do, it'll be in a kind of office, not a church. OK?"

He was crouching on the floor, buttoning up their denim jackets and helping them into their red knee-length wellingtons. They were going kite flying on Hampstead Heath. "But don't worry," he said. "You'll be sitting up front with us and wearing your Bus Stop gear. OK?"

It was clear that Julie, the bigger of the two and older by seven minutes, had no intention of being anywhere other than right at the front. She was permanently three inches taller than Chrissie and more forceful in every way. Although she was only eight, Julie had not only acquired a Welsh lilt and was a spit of Renée but, like her mother, she pushed and wheedled her way into everything, including her father's affections.

"But that's not fair!" Julie whined. "Mummy said we could be bridesmaids." Her face resembled an undercooked suet pudding, puffy and sweaty, her lips already sensual. "Mummy says Vanessa only ever thinks of herself and we won't be invited," she wailed. 'I hate Vanessa!' Mucus dribbled down onto her fleshy top lip and formed a little puddle there.

"Mummy said that?" Daniel was horrified. "Rubbish! Of course you'll be invited. You'll all come." Renée too I expect, he thought grimly to himself. What the hell was happening, he wondered.

"It's just that...you know...Vanessa would prefer a small wedding and not many people. You know?"

He stood up and shook the knees back out of his soft pink cord trousers, hitching them up to sit squarely on his hips.

"So let's just wait and see, shall we? We haven't even decided that we are getting married yet!" As he straightened his shoulders and tried to compose himself, Julie threw herself onto the floor and rolled over making her new cream leggings filthy.

"Mummy says that Vanessa doesn't like children," Chrissie sneered while wrenching at the legs and head of her Barbie-doll.

"Oh, for God's sake!" Daniel was losing it now. "Look, whatever happens, you'll be there and you'll be at the front with us. OK? So please just stop listening to what Mummy says about Vanessa. She really doesn't know her. Now, are we ready? Then let's go!"

With a dramatic wave of his arm he managed to both open the door and steer his daughters out in front of him, the beginnings of a migraine hovering over his right eye.

Downward Spiral

Two hours later, after dropping the girls back with Renée, he headed home and told Vanessa of their conversation about the wedding. She looked at him in horror.

"You WHAT? NO WAY! No way am I having those nightmare brats at our wedding. You know they'll do everything they can to spoil it! I bet *she* put them up to this. It's just the sort of thing she would do to cause as much trouble as possible. Welsh bitch." Vanessa was getting hysterical and felt a familiar wave of dread sweep over her.

"I'd rather not get married at all than have those two sneering and sniggering behind my back," she cried. "I'm sorry Daniel, but we agreed that if we got married there'd be no church, no hundreds of people and *definitely* no children! Just our immediate families and a few close friends; remember?" Her stomach was churning now. "You're not going to go back on that just to keep those two from whinging, are you? God, I just don't believe this!"

With mounting horror, Vanessa realised she was losing control of the situation. Up until then she had believed that Daniel had wanted the divorce as much as Renée; that he could no more live without Vanessa than she could without him. Having been named as co-respondent was fair enough, but she chose to believe he had only been sowing his wild oats before she came along and that now he was faithful to her. She was good at fooling herself and believing what men told her; they had pulled the wool over her eyes more times than she could remember. Even from when her father, Desmond, had walked out on her and Sofia. The problem was that she needed to be adored. Sofia's 'friend', Uncle Takis had worshipped her and treated her like a princess when she was little, so she had always felt like a precious jewel in his world, and that feeling was addictive.

Daniel pulled a face and rolled his eyes. This was starting to feel uncomfortably like the scenes he had had with Renée when they were married. What was it with women? Always creating problems. He pushed his chair back from the table, scraping it noisily on the dark patterned lino, grabbed his new leather coat from the sofa and headed towards the door.

"Where are you going?" demanded Vanessa, grabbing his shoulder and spinning him around.

"I'm taking the dogs to the Scrubs for a run." He stared down at her, his features rigid.

"Oh no you don't," she hissed, running round the table. She was getting red in the face. "You're not going to just walk off now in the middle of this. You're always doing that."

"They need a run; they haven't had a good run all week. We'll talk about it later."   He tried to keep calm as he moved awkwardly towards the door, his right arm pushing into the sleeve of his coat as he went. A fingernail caught on the lining and nearly ripped the delicate fabric.

"Shit! Look, I won't be long." He was getting irritated. His left arm was in now and he shrugged the expensive coat up and onto his shoulders, realising in a flash that he totally wanted out of the situation.

"Then I'm coming too," screeched Vanessa, her sleek, dark bob swinging wildly. She reached for her fake-pony-skin poncho hanging on the coat-stand and ran after him.

With his collar turned up, Daniel dug his hands deep into his pockets and sighed. They walked in silence along the main path of the Scrubs. He squirmed as his fingers clutched at the buttons of his beloved ankle-length coat. It was the colour of chocolate and as soft as butter, the lining an iridescent flash of turquoise silk. Vanessa had bought it for his last birthday and he knew he looked good in it; Australian Vicki had told him that too. The collar was made of fur, mink he believed. He had insisted on real fur, not artificial like on the hood of the poncho he had bought for Vanessa when she moved back to London. Hippy-happy Vicki loved to rub her cheek against the smoothness of his collar as they walked their dogs through the park. She would slip her arm through his and nuzzle her face into the soft, smooth fur. Of course, he knew that Vanessa would never understand this friendship so he had decided not to mention it. He just hoped that Vicki would not be there now, waiting for him, under their tree.

Vicki

Vicki temped all over central London and lived alone in a first floor conversion on the cheaper side of the Scrubs. She and Daniel had hit it off immediately. Although the initial attraction was physical, they had struck up a long conversation about the exercise needs of different breeds of dogs. She was a pretty but overweight 'flower-child' in her early twenties with bright auburn hair that parted in the middle and hung like a curtain to her waist. Her china blue eyes were lined with thick black kohl and spider-leg lashes got glued-on precariously each morning to the accompaniment of Pink Floyd at decibel ten on the radio. Purple lipstick framed sharp white teeth and, Daniel noted, her cheekbones were pure scaffolding. He had automatically started working out camera angles the moment he saw her.

"*Groovy* coat," she had sighed, moving closer. "Where'd you get it?"

"John Stevens - Carnaby Street," he replied. "Out shopping with my ex-girlfriend last month." Vicki nodded understandingly.

The dogs sniffed each other and charged around together as dogs do on first meeting. Before he knew what was happening she was inviting him round for coffee.

"Well, they get on really well together, don't they? I never knew big dogs could be so, you know, gentle…?" Her Australian accent fascinated him.

The next time Daniel saw Vicki she told him that her water heater had broken and she was wondering what on earth to do. She could take neither bath nor shower and certainly, on her secretary's salary, could not afford for someone to come and fix it. She wondered, glancing up at him shyly, did he know anything about these things, him being a photographer? Used to working with his hands? She was sure he'd know all about mechanical things?

"Well, *of course* I do," he said, puffing up and feeling pleased that she had asked him first. "Well, I know a fair bit."

In fact, he knew nothing about household things but he had been praying for a way in again so he could take some photos. He needed some new inspiration for his ongoing whipping-cream catalogue series and those cheekbones were a dream. That decrepit old water heater had dropped from the sky like a gift.

After that it became a regular thing. Daniel and Vicki would meet under the forked tree, walk quickly round the Scrubs one way - dogs running maniacally together with their tongues threatening to trip them up - turn and stroll more slowly round the other path, now arm in arm. Then, holding hands, they would run straight across the road to Vicki's pink and green bed-sit, maxi-coats flapping in unison. Daniel was well known in the area as a local boy who made good; the photographer who became famous for his trademark black and whites of barely-clad 'dolly' birds doing suggestive things with cans of whipping-cream. Instantly recognisable with his shoulder length blonde hair, tight blue jeans and leather coat that reached down to his snakeskin ankle boots, he was always slightly concerned that someone might see him and Vicki together and mention it to Vanessa. But he looked forward to their liaisons so much that after a while it did not even cross his mind that he might be found out. Of course, once they started having regular sex, he knew he had to be more careful.

The Forked Tree

As Daniel and Vanessa walked slowly round the perimeter of the Scrubs with Trixie and Jojo, avoiding mud and puddles, he knew he was rambling but felt unable to stop.

"Yeah, I do sometimes see Mrs Green here with Peggy. The vet said that she should be put down sooner rather than later - Peggy that is, not Mrs Green. Ha ha! The back legs are going and the dog's in pain..." He was sweating hard now and wishing he could take off his coat without Vanessa asking why on such a cold, wet day.

Vanessa made a sad face. "Poor Mrs Green, she'll be heartbroken. Oh look! Isn't that that Aussie girl you've mentioned a few times?"

"Eh? Who's that?" He wiped the back of his neck with his hand.

"You know, you told me. The fat Australian girl with the little Shih-Tzu dog. Over there by that funny tree. Looks like she's waiting for someone..."

"Erm. I don't know who you mean." He craned his neck in an exaggerated way.

"You *remember*, silly. You got chatting to her the day you wore your new coat for the first time. You said you thought she fancied you in it! Come on, let's go and talk to her." Vanessa grabbed his elbow and started dragging him towards Vicki.

"Oh, *her*! Er, yeeees - it could be. Oh, no. No. That's not her. No, her dog's bigger. Look, do you fancy seeing a film tonight? Because if you do..."

With his arm firmly around her shoulders he guided Vanessa away from where Vicki stood under the tree, soaking wet, her hair sticking in clumps to her face. Even from this distance he could see eye make-up running down her cheeks in thick, black rivulets.   "…we'd better go now or we'll be late.   OK? TRIXIE! JOJO! COME!"

Vicki could not understand what she was seeing, Daniel and a woman walking towards her and then abruptly turning and walking away?   She watched in horror from the shelter of the forked tree, her copper suede three-quarter-length darkening and pitting with every splat of rain.   She peered out from under the rim of her velvet fuchsia hat and sadly wondered how she was going to cope with knowing that Daniel had a new girlfriend.

Welsh Rarebit

In truth, Vanessa and Daniel had little concept of the vows they had taken. They simply knew in their hearts that by getting married they had made everybody happy but themselves. The fact that he was regularly sleeping with other women again was of no consequence to him. As long as Vanessa never suspected, there was no reason for it to be a problem, he decided.

On the surface, life was good. Their summer weekends were spent pottering about on 'Meg', the scrappy old barge they had dragged up from the bottom of the Thames at Windsor, and polished and painted till it sparkled like new. With Trixie and Jojo like figureheads at the helm, they would yank the cord of the motor and chug upstream to Henley or Marlowe and moor-up for lunch at one of the many riverside pubs. Everyone knew them along that stretch and treated them like royalty. Whenever Daniel had a fashion shoot Vanessa would go along and make herself useful, socialising and schmoozing and returning with a new list of phone numbers and contacts. Often on Saturdays they would shop in Kensington or Chelsea, then stay with rock-star friends in the country on Sundays. They moved in fashionable circles. Daniel was *the* fashion photographer most frequently being compared to Bailey, and Vanessa was getting her name known in the advertising world of Covent Garden.

Vanessa got her wish in that the wedding was small by celebrity standards, but as the filigree platinum band slipped onto her finger and she gazed into Daniel's eyes she felt a dull thud of panic. Oh, why had she let herself be talked into this? Both Sofia and Daniel's parents had voiced their unrelenting views that living together was a sin now that Daniel was divorced. But worse, her friends could not understand her fears; surely he was the 'catch of the century'? His pretty boy features were known in every trendy London restaurant, shop and club. Professionally, his star was in the ascendant. But, Vanessa argued, if he had cheated on Renée so often and so easily, what was to stop him doing the same with her? As he bent down to kiss her at the end of the wedding ceremony she felt like she had swallowed a brick. Hot tears welled up in her soft hazel eyes but she was determined to do her best and be the good wife that everyone expected. From that moment on, even though Vanessa sensed that Daniel was playing around, she decided to look the other way. But the Friday she arrived home from work early to cook a surprise Thai dinner, and found first-wife Renée in their bed, was the day she moved out.

As she dropped the shopping bags on the floor in the hall and walked slowly up the stairs, she wondered why the bathroom light was on. Passing it, she saw Daniel's naked body silhouetted against the frosted glass door. She continued walking up.

"You mean you didn't know?" smirked Renée, seeing the look of shock on Vanessa's face.

The ex-model was sitting up in bed smoking a black cigarette while Trixie and Jojo, either side of her, growled quietly. Heavy clumps of greasy blonde hair fell over her face as she talked, though she tried unsuccessfully to restrain it.

"Daniel said he'd told you and you were cool."

Renée's eyes were puffy and black mascara careered across her cheek. The oyster satin sheets that had taken Vanessa hours to choose in Biba the week before were heavily stained. She could not take her eyes off them.

"Thing is, Vanessa lurve..." that irritating Welsh voice of countless anonymous phone calls, "...we both know what we like, you know. We've known each other for so long. Anyway, I thought you wouldn't mind since he's screwing that fat Australian girl too."

Renée giggled, rolling over onto her stomach and propping herself up on her elbows. Vanessa could see she was wearing black patent leather boots and that the heels had ripped the bottom sheet.

"Oooh - you didn't know that either?" Renée squealed happily. "You're not going to cry, are you poppet? I'm so sorry, Vanessa lurve. Oooh, is this going to be a problem for you?" she pouted.

    Cigarette ash fell onto the bed as Renée half closed her eyes,
resting her cheek against the satin heart-shaped pillow. She peered
up at Vanessa through matted lashes.   They   both   heard
Daniel switch off the bathroom light, walk to the kitchen and open
the fridge.   Vanessa noticed a can of whipping-cream on the
bedroom floor, but no top.   The sweet stench of stale sweat hung
in the air. She leaned hard against the door-frame, and vomited.

5.
Spaghetti with Clams
- London -

1982

'La Bufala' restaurant was still run by first generation Italians from Campania and Alex told Liz that theirs was the best Spaghetti alla Vongole he had ever tasted. It was their first date so they both ordered it. He said he thought she would like it. She felt unsophisticated, and he seemed so familiar with the menu, that she was pleased to be led by him. From that day on Liz associated spaghetti and clams with Alex. The sweet garlic and oil combination of sauce and the occasional grittiness from the shells was all it would take to transport her back again to those happy times. Many years later, after having left Alex with the two boys when she could no longer cope, Liz moved around Italy alone. When the separation was at its most difficult for her, she would order the dish in an attempt to recreate the sensation of their love and their early days together. But Alex was right and she never did find the taste to be as good anywhere else as in 'La Bufula'.

Of course, back then, Liz had made the beginner's mistake of asking for grated cheese to be added but the owner of 'La Bufala', Giuseppe Salamida, refused and offered his masterpiece in the only way a true Italian could. He would never interfere with the pure and natural flavour of the seafood. Giuseppe explained that original seafaring cooks from the south of Italy knew what they were creating but it was the hearty Neapolitans, the indisputable pasta cognoscenti, who perfected the dish. One late night, without invitation, Giuseppe staggered exhausted to join Liz and Alex at their table and banged down a dusty label-less bottle and began reminiscing about the old days back home. He told of when he and his younger brother, Angelantonio, arrived in England. It was the summer of '52 and they had been working year after year on the family land until their fingers bled and their hearts had gone cold.

And of Rosa, their beautiful sister, who was betrothed to that monster Oronzo Scianni, a worker from a neighbouring farm. Her fate was sealed so she stayed behind in the little village, but at least she would never experience the 'exasperation, the gut-wrenching sadness' that her brothers did of 'living amongst culinary philistines!' Then, with a wide sweep of his arm, he scattered the plates across the table, put his head down on it and started quietly snoring. Liz and Alex never met Angelantonio.

So, for Liz, spaghetti with clams became indelibly linked to those magical Summer evenings with Alex. After finishing a hard day at the gallery, she'd kick off her shoes under the heavy round table and wriggle her toes, and delight in the sensation of tiny molluscs resting on her tongue. Alex understood wine and would order a wine of the white vermentino grape as he knew its slight mineral tang would enhance the whiff of brine in the dish before them. If he had signed up a new client that day, he would push the boat out and order a chilled Fiano de Avellino de Campagna, knowing that the distinctive white classic could not fail to hit the right romantic note. They would finish with a small fruit salad and perhaps a scoop of espresso granite topped with a dollop of cream. At this point, Liz would glance sideways at Alex and start twirling her hair around her fingers as he lounged back, hooking his thumbs into his belt. They knew when they had each other in the palms of their hands.

Liz soon realised that eating out was an essential part of Alex's lifestyle. As *the* art dealer of the moment, his world was fast becoming one of cocktail parties and schmoozing, lunches and expensive restaurants. They would often go to the Chelsea restaurant straight from work and sit on the noisy terrace and eat pasta; traffic fumes seasoning the food. Liz would spot Alex waiting for her on the nearby Kings Road corner, smooth-looking and relaxed and leaning up against the wall. With his ankles crossed, hands deep in jeans pockets and cool black Aviators balanced on his nose, his face would be turned upwards as if either napping or catching the disappearing rays of the sun. As she approached she would sense a momentary tension in his muscles as if he were suddenly aware of her presence, and he would drop his chin and turn to face her with those blank, black lenses. With that slow lazy burn that she got to know so well, his smile would start in one corner of his mouth and creep across his face like a soft wave of pure joy. Then he would grin like a kid. She was secretly thrilled he that was unable to control his feelings at those moments, or stay cool and detached any longer. His look said all his birthdays had come at once, and she felt she would burst with happiness. While barely moving a muscle he would elegantly extend an arm, his fine-fingered hand open, ready to take hers, and their flesh would spark as their skin made contact.

Come Autumn they would spend their time together picking at small delicacies in upmarket eating places around London: wild strawberries dipped in chocolate in Knightsbridge; tiny calamari in garlicky tomato with warm crusty bread in up-and-coming Notting Hill; champagne and cake in the dusty back streets of Camden Town, home to myriad antique shops; coffee and warm croissants - oozing butter - in stylish Islington; crab salad with hand-beaten home-made mayonnaise in gastro-famed Kew. But as Italy was synonymous with sex, for Liz it was spaghetti and clams that kept the fire burning and, later, the wound open.

From the beginning, Liz realised that food was more than just important to Alex Devlin. She had been observing him for months from her position on the gallery floor, as he brought in one new artist after another to meet Justin, her boss. Whereas most people would accept a coffee and nibble on a small biscuit out of politeness, Alex would pour extra cream into his cup and then scoff the expensive, Dutch buttery cookies one after the other, like a frantic chain-smoker going for a nicotine fix.

It was impossible to not hear him or ignore his conversations as she was as attuned to the sound of his voice as a mother is to her baby's cry. Liz knew the very moment he stepped out of a taxi outside the gallery and heard him pay the cabdriver. She felt her heart beat with the clang of the jaunty bell above the door as he made his way into the shop. Depending on where she was standing or what she was doing, she would pick up a file or a pile of papers and stride purposefully into the shop, expressing surprise and delight at seeing him again. It was her job to greet customers and she did it well, remembering their names, where they were from, their taste in art and when they were last in town. She realised Alex was becoming well-known in London, as much for his active passion for his work as an artists' agent as for his excessive party life-style. The fact that he was the best-looking hetrosexual man on the scene did not escape her either. But, even though Alex spent many afternoons in the gallery where Liz worked, it was a long time before she realised that he was as much in love with her as she was with him.

That day, instead of making his usual discreet entrance, Alex virtually fell in through the shop door. Liz had not heard his taxi outside, so was surprised and a little alarmed when she saw that he was drunk.

"Am I late?" he slurred, as he slammed the door shut behind him.

"Late, Alex? Late for what? You don't have an appointment today; it's Friday. Nobody comes in on a Friday, you know that." She continued tidying her papers and trying to act unconcerned.

"You mean no-one else is here? Thank God for that!" He collapsed into the pink and gold satin Louis XV chair by the door and proceeded to wrench off his shoes with his right hand.

"What are you doing, Alex? Are you drunk?" Liz was shocked. She had never seen the object of her desire and dreams behave in this way before.

"Drunk? No! Not really. Just a little. Ouch! Shit!" His left hand had been fishing around in a brown paper carrier bag on his lap and he pulled out the broken remains of a once-perfect bouquet of red roses. Blood oozed from his fingers and started to drip onto the rich, cream-coloured carpet. He threw the bag onto the floor and jumped to his feet.

"Quick! It's going everywhere! Oh, my God!" Liz ran to her desk and pulled out a box of white paper tissues. Grabbing the first, she shook it open and started dabbing at Alex's hand. Realising that the scratches were much deeper than she thought, she pulled the lot out and wrapped them round Alex's hand, totally enveloping it and holding it tightly at the same time. When she looked up he was staring at her and smiling.

"Wow! Will you marry me?" Liz laughed out loud and Alex started laughing too.

"You really are drunk, aren't you? What have you been up to?" She continued holding and dabbing at his hand. "And which flower shop did you steal those from?"

"They were for you," he said, sitting down heavily again. "Oh! I think I'm going to be sick!" She grabbed his arm and pulled him towards the back of the shop, rose petals and bits of bloody tissue falling all around them; like confetti, she thought. Pointing him towards the wash-room she ran back into the shop and picked up the debris in case someone did happen to break the Friday unspoken rule and arrive unexpectedly.

After sheepishly apologising over and over again before getting Liz to call a taxi to take him home to bed, Alex demanded her phone number and rang her the next day to ask her out.

6.
Too Many Ghosts
– Barcelona, Spain -

Steffie and Liam

Barcelona, 2007

Doing a double-take thinking she had seen Liam, Steffie stopped so absolutely still in the middle of the pavement that people had to curl around her like ice-skaters on a frozen pond. She was holding two plastic carrier bags of cushions in one hand and pulling a green tartan shopping trolley with the other. Having spent the past hour happily comparing tones of pink and purple, she had ended up by buying four cushions of completely different shape, size and colour combinations to take home and try out in her living room. Interestingly, as she was leaving the shop it occurred to her that these days she got a bigger thrill from buying home furnishings than clothes for herself. And then, as so often happened, stream-of-consciousness kick-started her backwards, dragging her along the path from currently furnishing her Barcelona apartment with killer-views of the city and sea to the last time she had been interested enough in improving her appearance to buy some clothes. Over the past ten years she had gained more weight that she ever thought possible. On and backwards to that original memory of knowing she would never see Liam again, and sitting down on the floor-cushion in her London loft mindlessly stuffing in every bit of food she could lay her hands on. Like a robot - an automaton. Blindly attempting to fill the un-fill-able space inside her where true love had firmly taken root.

Liam seemed to notice her at the same second, but it was impossible to tell what was going through his mind as the sun chose that moment to blast itself onto his naked face, and he put up his

hand to shade his eyes. Even though she could feel her legs turn to
the consistency of cold gravy, they propelled her towards his table.
He was only a short distance from where she had been standing but
time contorted and suddenly she was back in Holland Park sitting
on the grass with her arms around him. Everyone knows that
lovers become oblivious to their surroundings, but for her the
experience had been a revelation. It was as if they existed together
in a bubble; all sound around them having ceased except the calls of
the peacocks, all sight having disappeared but their smiles for each
other. He smelled of soap and shampoo and something else which
in time became familiar. When he crept up silently behind her and
put his hands over her eyes there was his smell, his unique and
personal signature, soft and clean and wonderful. She closed her
eyes briefly and breathed-in the memory of it.

       With a start, she found herself at his table looking down at
him, so familiar that she had to stop herself leaning forward and
kissing his face and hair, searching for his fingertips to hold against
her lips. Liam looked more like a blond Viking than ever with his
deep tan and shoulder length hair. He wore a loose blue cotton
shirt, neatly ironed and buttoned, the rolled sleeves skimming his
elbows and chosen - intentionally she suspected - to match the tint
of his eyes. Thick denim jeans were well-worn, 'broken in and
comfortable' he'd say; and tan leather boots that would have looked
more at home attached to the legs of a cowboy than a city-break
tourist.

       "Liam? Is it you?" Her voice trembled unrecognisably.
       "Yes, it's me."
       She had no idea what to say next.
       "Are you alone?"
       "I am."
       She sat down heavily on the white plastic chair opposite
him, clutching her carrier bags for stability and searching his face
for a clue, like a hypnotist choosing an accomplice for a stage act.

       A good-looking waiter came out of a building close by and
quick-stepped over to where they were sitting, wiping his hands on
his apron and expertly dodging the human traffic on the pavement.

       "Si?" he drawled, barely looking at her.
       Steffie's mind went blank. "What did he mean, si? Si
what?"

Was this not the day she had dreamed of for years? "Si –
claro!" Was this not the scenario she had gone through in her head
a million times in case the only man she had ever loved happened
to find himself in Barcelona on the street she happened to be
walking down at that moment? Si?

Si! Si, si, si, si, si - of course! Steffie gazed into the young
man's bored olive-brown face as if he might have the answer to all
life's problems.

"Si. Una cerveza, por favor."

The shaven-headed waiter attempted to wipe the grubby
round table with a small cloth that appeared as if by magic, but
moved it over the top so quickly it missed most of the sticky
surface. He then turned on his heel and disappeared into the
cheerless interior of the bar. Liam and Steffie sat there looking at
each other, not knowing what to do or say next. He held his head
slightly to one side as if listening for something, but his eyes held a
question.

"So, Steffie. You came here then. You always said you
would." He smiled and the tension in his face evaporated and his
sea-blue eyes sparkled. "I must admit," he continued "that
although I often thought I might - I never quite believed I'd see you
- by chance - you know - in the street somewhere like this."

She could feel hot tears welling up behind her eyes like the
threat of a summer storm about to break. Her vision misted and
she swallowed hard.

"I couldn't stay in England any longer," she finally said.
"Too many ghosts. You know. Too many memories."

Steffie looked away and noticed three young Japanese
tourists standing on a mosaic bench having their photo taken by a
man who was crouching on the ground. The girls were young and
pretty and he was encouraging them to lift their already short skirts
even higher.

"Sorry, w-what did you say?" she mumbled, looking back at
him.

"I said that that was my line – too many ghosts!"

She smiled weakly and felt her heart splinter.

Suddenly the waiter was back, delicately positioning a
foaming glass of beer onto a cardboard Pepsi coaster and smiling at
her and acting friendly. Just as it seemed he was going to ask for
the money, his attention was taken by a tall tanned slim-hipped boy

who glided past in expensive white linen and clutching a portfolio of what looked like photos. As Steffie watched the young men lock eyes, a steamy non-verbal conversation ensued between them in the seconds it took the boy to walk past. Suddenly the waiter was gone, so she turned back to the table and determinedly picked up her beer.

"Salud!" she cried, with more insouciance than she felt, releasing one of the carrier bags to the pavement.

"Slainte!" Liam replied.

"Na Zdrowie!"

"Kanpai!" Steffie giggled, leaning back in her chair and letting go of the other bag.

"Prosit!"

"Za vashe zdorovye!" She burst out laughing.

"A votre sante!" she screamed.

"Ooogy Wawa!" Liam yelled back into her face, grinning.

All eyes were on them but who cared? She felt as drunk as if she had been knocking them back all morning.

Steffie lifted up her glass and roared, "May yer pockets be heavy and yer heart be light." The words rushed out before she could stop them, weighted with the Irish lilt he had schooled her in.

"An' may good luck pursue yer each mornin' an' night," he whispered back.

Lunchtime traffic shuddered past and they sat there looking at each other without speaking. Steffie turned her face to the sun and closed her eyes, allowing the tears to dry on her cheeks. Liam always was good at silences, she thought - comfortable just sitting there; no need to talk. Not like her, who had to fill every gap.

She opened her eyes to see him watching her, determined not to be the first to speak - to break the spell.

"So why are *you* here?" she gave in. "Holiday or work?"

Liam smiled. She sensed he was remembering the way she used to be; and how he would tease her and call her a 'terrible woman' whenever she could not stop talking. Or he would roll his eyes and laugh, which infuriated her. But really, she loved it. She loved Liam. Sometimes after sex, Steffie would have nothing to say or, if she did, she had no strength left to say it. That was when he said he loved her the best, when she was quiet and happy and satisfied. And that was when he would start talking of Ireland and stammering about his childhood; of his father, Gerard, coming home drunk, barely able to stand, and cruelly annihilating his drawings and childish poetry. "Jaaysus! What the fock is thaat! Can this be a son of moine, woman?" Liam would tell of how his mother used him as a substitute for her husband's lack of desire, and that if only he had dared speak to the boys in class how he might have discovered that he was not the only son to be abused in this way. Instead, the humiliation of what he was forced into left him with scars so deep that he only felt safe exposing them after making love with this woman sitting opposite him now; the one he said he cared more for than anyone else in the world. He would speak and Steffie would listen and say nothing and never judge. More than once he whispered that she was his healing medicine, his 'rescue remedy' he called her. All the more reason then why what he referred to as her 'betrayal' scorched him to the very soul and ultimately turned him from her.

Liam and Steffie

Barcelona, 2007

Liam sat there gazing at her adored profile and felt his stomach lurch. Jeezus - she was jawing with that waiter again, and in Spanish. She knew he could not understand what they were saying and in a second all the old feelings were back: the insecurities and doubts. He shifted uncomfortably in his chair and looked away. A gaggle of schoolgirls wearing grey and red uniform were dancing around what was probably their teacher but could equally have been a student on his gap year, he looked so young. Steffie and the greasy-looking waiter were laughing together, like old friends Liam thought when he looked back, and he noticed the way the skin round her eyes wrinkled as she smiled at the smarmy Spaniard. She obviously still liked them young. Ten years has made little difference to her, he mused, but what must she be thinking when she looks at himself? He kept himself pretty fit, his job with the horses saw to that, but he knew the damage that the Texan sun was doing to his skin; he just never got around to checking things out. Out on the open range with space enough around him to think deep thoughts and lose the past, it seemed unimportant. There he managed to forget everything but the moment: the stillness of the air, two bald eagles circling in the azure sky overhead, hard red earth, the warmth of the sun and the rich smell of the animals.

Sitting here though, on the elegant Barcelona street, Liam vowed that when he got back he would drive into town and have someone take a look at the strange black shapes forming on his neck and hands. But first he had to finish up this trip to Europe.

In his heart he knew it would be his last, old friends in London and Belfast having moved on or died. Or just lost touch. Ma's funeral last week was a strange affair with so few people turning up. Sure, they made all the right noises and kept up the banter but Liam had always known that people around had hated his father and despised his mother. More than one familiar face that day came up and told him the best thing he ever did was to go across the water to England. He remembered one Christmas Day when Da had done the right thing too, by dropping dead. Sitting in his chair as fat as the turkey roast and rashers he had gorged, with all the trimmings he had insisted on and bullied Ma into staying up all night to prepare. Bastard. Served him right and gave us all a good day off.

Steffie was speaking again now and asking where Liam lived. He had forgotten how clear and light her voice sounded.

"Well, why don't you guess?" London? Ireland? She could not.

"What? You mean you really did go to Texas? You live in America now?"

Her face was crumpling by the second and he just wanted to take her in his arms and hold her there forever.

"So why should you care?" Liam shifted in his seat and crossed his legs, directing them away from her body. "You have your young Spanish waiters. Sure there's plenty here to keep you occupied." Liam knew what he was doing but could not stop himself. It was eating away at him like it used to; he just could not let her off the hook. As he had said to Sean, his closest friend, better to do it to her first, because sure as eggs is eggs she'll do it to me. Well, he was right, because she did do it, and with her pretty-boy student. She never actually admitted it, and Liam was not absolutely sure but he was pretty sure: she looked so dammed guilty anyway. Thing is, she did not deny it. Liam pushed his chair backwards on the pavement, stood up and pulled a roll of fresh euro notes from his pocket.

"Perhaps you could ask your friend how much I owe him for the drinks. I'm sure you want to make some plans for later too. Well, don't let me cramp your style. I've got to be on me way. I've things to do."

Steffie sat and stared at him. For the second time that day he saw tears spring to her eyes, but this time there was a look of such deep sadness and pity that it was all he could do to not look away. OK, so why should he be the only one to suffer? When she left, she made him more miserable than he'd ever been in his entire life. Well, he thought, now I've gotten the land and the horses; and sure they won't turn round and hurt me.

Epilogue

Barcelona, 2007

Liam took a step backwards and combed the fingers of his sunburnt hands through his still-thick shoulder length hair, white-bleached and dried by the sun, the way he used to, she thought, when it was newly wet from the shower.

"Well. Gotta be going I guess. Look after yourself. And who knows, if you're ever out in Texas..." He winked the way he always used to when he left her and, with the sentence trailing like the closing line of a bad movie, he walked off into the sea of tourists staring open-mouthed at the balconies of Gaudí's Casa Batlló.

Steffie continued sitting there, surrounded by her bags now spilling out their bruised contents onto the pavement as the waiters changed shifts. The sun went down and gangs of 'hens' in baby-doll pyjamas and with phallic-shaped dummies hanging round their necks appeared on the street for their last-night piss-up before settling down to married life.

7.
Spiralling in Reverse
- Spain -

Daughters
Barcelona, 2007

Early morning noises in the building made Steffie groan as she rolled onto her back and tried to open her eyelids. The already-brilliant sun streamed through the green shutter slats of her bedroom window towards her sore, encrusted eyes. Automatically, she pulled the duvet tight up to her chin, trapping the warm air inside the bed. Immediately she remembered. Each waking moment felt like a weight on her heart as sadness enveloped her again. Her shoulders ached from the locked-in tightness around her muscles. She never thought she could cry so much but, from the day Liam turned up and then walked out of her life again, Steffie felt she had spent more time weeping than in her whole life before. She felt a mess and knew but did not care how bad she looked and smelled. Her face was puffy and her nose red raw from wiping it. In her more lucid moments she wondered how much liquid could possibly be left in her body. She had kept herself in a state of near coma by sleeping and was physically exhausted and emotionally wrecked. Steffie wanted to just die and put an end to her suffering and pain.

She jumped as a large bluebottle crashed against the glass of the window, trapped inside the room and desperately seeking a way out. Steffie watched it hurl itself against the glass, over and over, frantically buzzing then dropping to the floor for a few seconds, only to gather up its strength and start again. Feeling a connection between herself and the fly she wondered when it would give up completely. Surely it could see there was no escape? Why not give in gracefully and resign itself to its fate? The bluebottle could see freedom beyond the transparent crystal barrier but it did not realise

that it could not break through.   Steffie closed her eyes again
wondering why she felt no sympathy for the trapped fly.   She had
always been acutely aware of the suffering of animals; even insects
had her support.   She would find just the right receptacle to capture
them and the right piece of paper to slide between that and the wall
or floor, then carefully carry all to the open door and release the
desperate creature back to its natural environment.   Much as she
disliked and even feared spiders, she could not kill one.   She once
even slept on the sofa in the living room with the door shut rather
than harm one enormous black monster high up on her bedroom
wall, until help arrived the next morning.

     In fact, Steffie had spent her life caring for animals and
people, never consciously harming a living thing, always aware of
suffering, always tuned-in to the needs of others.   But here she was
now alone, uncared for herself, dying inside with nobody to know
or even care that she existed.   In that moment she realised she
missed her mother.   More than anything she needed to feel
Vanessa's strong arms around her shaking body, her cool mother's
hands stroking her damp forehead and hair, soft fingertips wiping
her swollen eyes.   Steffie lay rigid in bed, straight and still like a
corpse, wishing for release.   She decided to will her body to close
down, bit by bit.   Overwhelmed by grief and loneliness she started
to whimper then whine like an abandoned dog.   As the sound got
louder it became a scream, from a place so deep within that she did
not recognise it as coming from herself.   From the core of her pain
she screamed, the sound intensifying by the second.   Again and
again it burst from her, building uncontrollable momentum until
finally there was nothing.   She felt her energy leave, like a
malevolent spirit exorcised from her body, and in that moment she
knew she had died.   Now she was still; relaxed and empty of grief.
She felt clean, new and reborn.

     Steffie started to laugh at he absurdity of having died so
easily and could not believe how different she felt.

     "Wow!" she thought. "This is great. I've done it."

     The pain had gone, the sadness, the sense of loss and
abandonment.   She sat bolt upright and her shoulders dropped and
relaxed as the tension drained away.   She glanced around the room
and saw the bluebottle on its back on the floor, valiantly trying to
get a foothold and resume its attempt at escape.   She looked around
for something to trap it in and spotted a wineglass, encrusted red,

from several days before. In one move she was out of bed and sprinting across the room. Grabbing the glass and placing it over the damaged bluebottle, she decided it would be OK to leave it there until she could find some paper to slide underneath before transporting the whole ensemble to the balcony door and setting the lucky creature free. Steffie never felt more alive and well. This caused her to laugh again since she was convinced she was dead. It was a miracle how good she felt! She automatically made her way towards the bathroom, surprised how full her bladder felt. After relieving herself, she started to question if she really was dead. She decided to try to make a phone call and find out, so she picked up the phone and, instantly recalling the number she had not dialled for over ten years, called her mother.

Mothers
Madrid, 2007

Vanessa had been having a bad time too, recently. Her clients sat and poured out their troubles to her on a weekly basis but, of course, had no idea of her own unhappiness. No idea of who she was, of anything about her life: her highs, lows and disappointments. Ever the professional, she listened and empathised but kept an objective stance. But right now Vanessa was sitting at her favourite table in the plaza having her morning coffee. She was feeling good, alive and in control: powerful. After ten turbulent years, she had finally told Manuel it was over and he had left immediately, his Spanish pride preventing him staying another moment where he was not wanted. She ordered a pastry to celebrate.

She was wearing a simple linen shift dress, expensive and black. Around her neck was the white silk scarf that Alex had left with her as a momento of her cousin Jack. She wished she could have given it to Steffie as a keepsake, but they had rowed about Manuel and she had not seen her daughter since she left Madrid ten years ago. Steffie was a stubborn girl and had refused to give her mother her address in Barcelona. 'She sure knows how to dish it out,' thought Vanessa, 'and how to keep turning the screw.' While she waited for the waiter to return with her pastry, which she was already starting to feel guilty about, Vanessa sat fingering the scarf and thinking back to that argument. Vanessa liked things of quality, and things that had history and meaning.

She had gone to the gym early and was now fresh from the shower, her auburn hair still damp, combed back and slick. Feeling emotionally strong that day, she had decided to leave off her make-up and face the world 'au natural'. She had already noticed the good-looking older man several tables away and knew he had been eyeing her for some time too. Mid-grey hair curling to the collar and brushed straight back from a taurine forehead; face, hands and ankles golden tanned, soft suede beige loafers and well-cut beige trousers with leather belt, an expensive-looking white shirt with the cuffs turned back to his elbows. He wore an elegant gold ring on the little finger of his right hand and a heavy-looking watch hung loosely from his left wrist. His eyes were hidden behind rimless sunshades. Out of the corner of her eye she saw him beckon the waiter and pay his bill, pick up his keys and newspaper and rise from his seat.

'Oh, shame,' she thought, 'he's going. Just my luck.' Then, 'Oh, my god!' She swallowed hard. 'He's walking this way. He's coming towards me.'

Vanessa pretended to study her mobile phone and tapped meaningless numbers into it while aware that he was circumnavigating the tables. She leaned back and crossed her legs elegantly, putting the phone to her ear with her left hand while steadying herself with her right against the leg of the table. She glanced up at him enquiringly as he rested both his hands on the top of her table and leaned forwards. His sunglasses were now perched comically on his nose, giving the impression he was peering over them at her, like a librarian or schoolteacher. She noticed the deep dimple in his chin.

"I see that you are a very beautiful woman," he stated. His voice was low and heavily accented. He smelled of something woody and fragrant. "May I ask – why are you dressed like you've been to a funeral? Have you?" His eyes twinkled and she caught a flash of turquoise behind heavy black lashes before she allowed herself to be outraged at his audacity.

"I beg your pardon?" she spluttered. "Are you talking to me?"

He stood upright again and looked around him in a comical and exaggerated way.

"I believe I must be, since there's no-one else here. May I sit down and comfort you in your grief?" Without waiting for an answer, he expertly twirled the chair round and straddled it, so his knee gently nudged against hers.

"So, my dear, who was it that died? Was it your husband, or perhaps a favourite lover? Or maybe your dog got old?"

Vanessa sat staring at him with her mouth agape, unable to pull herself together or think of a single thing to say.

"You see," he continued, barely drawing breath, "there are only two reasons that an English woman as beautiful as you would be so careless with her appearance. They are: one, due to the death of someone or something close (more likely, an animal), and two, because someone has mistakenly informed her that to wear so shapeless an outfit, no make-up and with hair straight from the shower would make her look striking, bold and sexy. If the second is correct," he continued mockingly, hypnotically holding her gaze, "and I suspect it is, my dear madam I feel it is my duty, in the name of all red-blooded men over the age of 16, to put the record straight." With that, he snapped his fingers at a passing waiter and ordered two glasses of champagne.

Vanessa, could hardly trust herself to speak, she felt so humiliated.

"How did you know I was English?" was all that came out.

He grinned triumphantly and she caught a flash of gold. The waiter returned with two flutes of champagne on a small, round tray. With a flourish and a whispered aside of 'Suerte!', he placed the glasses and a small white bowl of olives down between Vanessa and her new friend who, to her horror, winked at the waiter as he thanked him.

"Oh, I get it," she said slowly. "You own the place."

"Madam, please!" Now it was his turn to be outraged. "I would never own such a run-down establishment. I am simply a customer, like yourself, but well-known for demanding and getting the best."

He picked up one of the glasses, handed it to Vanessa and holding the other aloft whispered, "A toast: to departed husbands, virile ex-lovers and devoted dogs. May they all rest in peace!"

He clinked his glass against hers and took a deep swallow. Vanessa felt herself softening to this ridiculously amusing man and took a sip.

"That's better!" he beamed. "Now, madam, allow me to introduce myself. Carlos María Eduardo García de la Cal Fernández Leal Luna Delgado Galván Sanz, at your service!" She was not sure, but she thought she heard him click his heels. "And you, madam? Who do I have the pleasure of addressing, please?"

Vanessa had taken a few sips and was starting to enjoy herself. She played with the stem of her glass and wondered exactly what it was he wanted of her. First he had complemented her by saying she was beautiful, and then he had insulted her by telling her she looked drab.

"Actually," she started, "I must tell you. First, I'm not a tourist. I live here." She saw the sparkle leave his eyes. "And second, I speak Castellano." He looked at her in mock horror.

"Yes. And so I'm wondering why the waiter wished you 'good luck' just now? Am I right in thinking," she was getting bolder, "that you come here regularly on the look-out for a wife?" Now his look of horror was genuine.

"Oh, no, no, NO, madam. A new wife is absolutely the last thing I want."

"Aha! So in that case it's a younger girlfriend you're after. Your wife is getting too old for your *tontarías*, is that it? You have a daughter of my age and you want to be seen out with a younger woman now your wife's a bit long in the tooth, eh? Huh!" In looking away from him, Vanessa managed to make her feeling of disgust quite plain.

Her companion sat more upright than ever, put his hand on his heart, smiled and looked Vanessa straight in the eye.

"My dear, you have absolutely the wrong idea about me. The reason I came over to talk was because you looked so sad and bored, like you needed some fun. I thought to myself, Carlos, there's an English rose over there who needs your services." He paused. "Having known and loved many, many English flowers in my time – in fact only last week I met some delightful twin sisters from Lowestoft, here on holiday for a few days – I believe I understand what makes them tick, as you say, and what they need to make their short stay in my beautiful city complete. If I can have a little fun at the same time, of course..."

The penny clunked so suddenly and obviously that Vanessa could not believe that she had not realised before exactly what Carlos María Eduardo García de la Cal Fernández Leal Luna Delgado Galván Sanz had in mind.

She started to wonder how much he would charge for his 'services' if they went back to her apartment, now that Manuel was gone. As she was on the point of asking him, the waiter returned to their table and passed her new friend a small, folded piece of paper. Carlos drew his hands to his chest to open it discreetly, all the while tilting his head to show that he was still listening to her, ever the professional. He glanced down once, scanned it quickly and nodded to the waiter, who scuttled back inside.

"My dear," Carlos said gently but formally. "This has been delightful and I wish I could stay longer, but I had completely forgotten that my niece from New York was arriving and is waiting inside for me. I simply must go. Please, finish your champagne and, who knows, maybe our paths will cross again one day."

With that, he stood up and swayed a little. Leaning forward he picked up Vanessa's hand, lifted it to his face and expertly brushed his lips across her fingers. He then turned and walked quickly inside.

Vanessa sat as if in a state of shock. Had all that really happened? As she drank down the last remaining drops of champagne, her mobile phone rang. Without checking the number, as she normally would, she opened it up to hear her daughter Steffie's voice, like a ghost from the past.

"Mama? Mama? Is that you?"

Born and raised in Richmond near London, Jean Gilhead has been writing short stories since she was a child. After travelling to many countries, she put roots down in Spain and now divides her time between Barcelona and London. Working as a life-style  coach and presentations skills trainer, Jean Gilhead can be contacted through her website: www.bestmoveforward.com. Bilingual, she is a self-taught writer: *Living in Bright Shadows* is her first full-length novel.

All the characters in this book are fictitious.

Printed in the United States
131763LV00005B/247/P

9 781849 231534